A PRINCESS FOR THE GENTLEMAN

UNLIKELY MATCH SERIES

MINDY BURBIDGE STRUNK

ACKNOWLEDGMENTS

Acknowledgements: To Jenny Proctor, my always fabulous editor who even edited this book the week before Christmas because I am a crazy person and thought that was good idea. Thanks for all the help.

To my proof-readers- Patti Knowlton, Ronda Freed, Lorraine Gwilliam, Wilma Bishop and Michelle Pomeroy who always catch those last minute errors. Thanks a bunch!

For my great writers' group: Dickens, Heyer, Bronte and Austen! Thanks for replying to my random messages and gifs about nothing. Thanks for listening when I rant. And thanks for being there when I just need the support because this writing gig is hard. You are truly my best friends!

To my great ARC team. Thank you for all you do to help me be successful! I couldn't do it without you guys.

Thanks to the rest of my extended family who sees me a lot less since I started publishing consistently. Your support is appreciated.

And last and most importantly, for all my boys. Thanks for not complaining when you want to do something and I keep saying 'just let me finish this chapter.' Thanks for telling your friends and teacher that your mom is a really good writer and promoting my books to them. And for encouraging me—telling me I 'made a good job choice to become an author.' I love you, tons! Especially to my biggest boy, Christopher for continuing to support my crazy goals and my endless 'sweats days'. I couldn't do this without. LY

CHAPTER 1

Dugray Dawson reined in his horse, pulling it to a stop. He gathered his greatcoat around him tighter, blocking out the wind sweeping across the open fields. "The land has potential, I will give you that, Tad. But the house—it will need a complete renovation. Most of it is not habitable and the dower house? I am surprised it is still standing."

Tad Wentworth glanced over at his friend. "But I believe parts of the house are livable. Perhaps it is not the luxury some might expect, but one could live in it while making the repairs on other parts of the house."

Dawson shook his head. "What I do not understand is why you wish to purchase it. Compared to Morley Park, this place is a hovel. Why should you even consider it?"

Tad shrugged. "Once it is repaired it could be let for a handsome price." He gazed sideways at Dawson.

Dawson narrowed his eyes at the Duke of Shearsby, knowing that look. He had seen it many times in his lifetime and it never led to anything good. This, he was sure, would not be an exception.

"Or someone else could buy it..." Tad left the sentence dangling.

Dawson let out a grunt-groan. "What have you done, Tad?"

A large smile spread across Tad's face. "Nothing so very bad. I only put money down to hold the estate. I did not wish to have someone else sweep in and snatch it from under our noses. After all, it is rare for a property such as this to come available. I did not want your excessive thinking to interfere and cause us to miss out."

The duke surely had a plan. He always had a plan. And they almost always involved Dawson, somehow. Dawson swept his hand in front of him. "Out with it. I know you have a grand notion you wish to share with me. Lay it out so I can decline, and we can get out of this blasted cold." He shifted in his saddle, trying to relieve the ache in his hips. When had he gotten so old? Was three and thirty so very old? His body told him it was.

Tad's horse danced in place, throwing his head back several times. Even the animals were cold and wished to return to Morley Park.

Tad set his horse in motion back toward the manor house. "I thought, perhaps, you could purchase the place."

Dawson opened his mouth to refute such a preposterous plan, but Tad went on, completely ignoring him.

"As I said, parts of the house are livable. Come spring, we can make the necessary repairs to the roof and rockwork outside. Then you may make the interior repairs at your leisure."

Dawson scrubbed a hand over his face. He used the word *we*, but what he meant was Dawson. Dawson could make the repairs. Dawson could live in the hovel.

He pulled his horse to a stop and interjected while Tad took in a breath. "But there is already a flaw in your plan. I do not have the money to buy this place." He folded his arms across his chest, satisfied with himself for putting an end to the discussion before it had even begun. But then his brow crinkled. It was not like Tad to have a plan fall apart so early into it.

As he thought, Tad only smiled at him, pulling ahead of Dawson and calling over his shoulder. "But you do. With the money I know you have saved and the money I have put away for you—"

Dawson dug his heels into Ares's flanks. "Wait just a moment. What money you have put away for me?"

"Do you not remember when first we came to Morley Park and I offered you a salary to be my secretary? You told me it was an excessive amount and refused it, instead agreeing to only half the amount?" Tad shrugged. "I have been paying the other half into the bank for these last two years. It has grown into quite a respectable sum. By my calculations, if you used both savings, and what you brought with you from America, you would have enough to buy this place, with enough left over to buy at least a half-dozen horses."

Dawson closed his gapping mouth, his teeth aching as the heat from inside his lips warmed them. "Why am I buying a half-dozen horses?"

"To breed, of course. One cannot be a horse breeder without horses." Tad looked on Dawson as if he were daft.

Dawson stared at him, blinking several times as the wind dried out his eyes. "I am to be a horse breeder? When did I decide this?" His voice was gruff and clipped.

Tad laughed. "You have been thinking on it for some time. And I, for one, think it a brilliant idea."

"It takes time to become a breeder, Tad. How am I to support this estate, let alone have enough money to make the needed repairs?"

Tad nodded. "Not to worry. You have this planned out as well."

Dawson looked at him with a bland expression, his head throbbing at his temples. He should have known this would be a lengthy plan. Tad never did anything by halves. "I have been very busy, thinking, have I not?"

"Did I not say you thought excessively much?" Tad grinned. "First we will repair the tenant cottages."

Dawson snorted. "*We?* I do not think it proper for the Duke of Shearsby to be mending tenant cottages. Mending the ones on your own estate caused murmuring enough. I can only imagine what gossip will follow if you are seen atop my tenant cottages."

"You have begun to think of this place as yours. Very good." He dropped from his horse and tethered it to a nearby tree before striding up the steps to the terrace of the manor house. He turned to Dawson and Tad's smile faltered. "We have long established that I am not a typical English Duke. We mended the cottages at Morley; we will do it here at Fawnbrooke, unless you choose to rename it."

Dawson shook his head. "I have no notion of what I would change it to."

They pushed into the front entryway. Wallpaper hung in tattered clumps from the walls, and plaster was chipped and missing from the ceiling above. Cobwebs strung from one branch of the chandelier to the next.

Dawson pushed out a long, slow breath through his teeth. What was Tad thinking? This place was a wreck.

Tad took the stairs two at a time and Dawson reluctantly followed, turning down the darkened corridor. Tad opened each door, peering inside. "It appears most of the bed chambers in the east wing just need a good cleaning and perhaps some paint. "Yes, I think this is very encouraging."

Dawson looked into the first room. Perhaps this could be his mother's room. An unexpected warmth filled him.

They moved to the end of the corridor and Tad threw open the door to a large room. "This must be the master's rooms."

Dawson walked in and turned around. A door on the left led to the dressing room, which was positioned between this room and another of exact measurements. The second would obviously belong to the mistress of the house. Dawson grunted. Would there even ever be a mistress? It seemed unlikely and his chest tightened at the thought. Had he wholly given up on the notion of finding a suitable match? He pushed the thought away for now and returned to the corridor, waiting for Tad to shut the door behind them.

"It seems to me if you shut off the West Wing until we make the repairs, you should be able to live comfortably enough here." Tad clapped his hands together and wiped them against each other, trying to remove the dust and dirt.

Dawson stared at his friend. Tad was completely serious. He thought this plan a good one. Dawson did not know what to think. He scratched at the back of his neck. So many things could go wrong. What if he lost it all? What if it turned out he was like his father?

Tad walked back to the front doors and stepped out into the cold. He motioned to the land they had just surveyed. "As I was saying, if we are able to rent the cottages before spring, you will be able to have that income to help until the horses start to turn a profit." He scrunched his mouth up to one side. "I confess, in your plan, you will be living in the east wing of the house for several years. But you felt it a necessary sacrifice for a successful future." He gave a little chuckle, obviously amused by his own wit.

Dawson leaned his elbows on the stone wall that lined the front terrace. At one point it had likely been grand, Dawson was sure, but it now crumbled in several places. He looked out over the land from an owner's perspective. It was impressive land. There was much that could be grown here, and the sections which were too rocky for vegetation could easily support sheep or cattle. He had dreamed of owning his own farm again, had yearned for it. His dream usually had him back in Pennsylvania, but with his mother soon to arrive, he knew returning to the United States was not likely anymore. "Do you really believe this is a feasible plan, Tad?"

Tad moved in close, joining Dawson with elbows on the wall. "I would not have brought it to you if I did not."

A fluttering erupted in Dawson's stomach and his hands shook, suddenly damp inside his thick, woolen gloves. Even thinking about doing such a thing was lunacy, was it not? It was easy for Tad to believe such grand things possible. He was a Duke with great financial security. But Dawson? He did not have the luxury to gamble on such endeavors. If it failed? His chest felt tight and he found each breath more difficult than the last. This was too much, too soon.

"I need to think on it." He pushed himself away and bounded down the stairs, practically leaping onto his horse.

Tad jogged to keep up. "As I knew you would. Which is precisely why I put the money down. We have until month's end to make the decision. Then we either pay the remaining money or have the money I put down returned." He looked hard at Dawson. "I think this is a good opportunity, Dawson. One that does not come along often. The land is good which makes it a lower risk."

"If you think the land will support the estate, why even bother with the breeding?"

Tad turned his horse back in the direction of Morley Park and Dawson followed as they began the five-mile journey back.

"I believe the land will only just support the estate, but it will never get you ahead. You will always be living from one harvest to the next, hoping nothing catastrophic happens to bring everything down around you." He paused. "Besides, you are the best horseman I know. It only seems natural for you to take up breeding. You will make a success of it. Of that I have no doubt."

Dawson remained silent, thinking on his friend's words. It was hard not to feel Tad's same confidence after hearing his speech. "I will think on it while fetching my mother from Liverpool next week."

Tad grinned. "She is to arrive next week? I can hardly believe it is so soon." He leaned slightly forward in his saddle. "You know, the Earl of Somerton is selling the offspring of his stallion, *Eclipse*. The earl's estate would only be a day or two out of your way on your return from Liverpool. Perhaps you could stop and buy the horse then."

"I have not yet decided to agree to your plan, Tad. I am wondering if I should be committed to Bedlam for even considering it." Dawson frowned.

Tad shrugged. "I am most excited to see your mother again. It has been too long." He took a long breath. "I confess, I had hoped my mother and sisters would have come already."

Dawson nodded. He understood the loneliness that crept in. Although, Tad had Violet to keep his loneliness at bay. Dawson had no one—except Tad. But Tad could not fill the void left inside Dawson when he had departed for England and his mother had stayed behind in Pennsylvania. Yes, it would be good to have her here at last.

They stopped in front of the stables at Morley and a boy came running out. Dawson and Tad dismounted almost in unison, handing over the reins.

"The proximity to Morley I believe to be advantageous as well." Tad started up the stairs.

"I am certain there will be times when it will feel too close," Dawson muttered.

Tad glanced back over his shoulder, smiling even as his head shook.

The front door opened, and Baker nodded to them as they stepped over the threshold. They both stopped as the warmth of the house settled over them.

Violet, the Duchess of Shearsby, appeared at the top of the stairs. She walked quickly, with more grace than Dawson would have thought possible.

She took hold of Tad's hand, wrapping her other arm around his. Going up on tiptoe, she pressed a kiss to his cheek before dropping back down to flat feet. "Well, did he agree?"

Dawson's chest tightened. He did not desire Violet for himself; he never had. But he did desire what she and Tad had—the love they felt for each other.

Tad placed his free hand over hers. "As I suspected, he wishes to think on it."

Violet smiled at Dawson. "Dawson is a wise man. I think him prudent not to rush into anything."

Dawson gave a slight shake of his head. Perhaps it would be good for him to get away from Morley, away from the daily reminder of what he did not have, and with every passing day, did not believe he ever would.

CHAPTER 2

*Z*ia Petrovich fastened a serviceable woolen cloak around her shoulders, shoving her fingers into her gloves. She frowned at the mousy colored frock. Did Tiana not have something better?

"Are you sure this is necessary?" Tiana asked as she fastened Zia's heavy, ermine-trimmed cloak at her throat. "Why must I pretend to be you, *knyázhna*? Do you think it possible word has reached England of your arrival?" Tiana's English was broken and accented. Thankfully, it would not change the plan. Not all members of the Russian imperial family spoke English as well as Zia.

Zia scowled at her maid. "You are not to call me princess here. How many times must I repeat this, Tiana?"

Zia sighed. Sometimes she wondered if Tiana had a brain in her brainbox. Was it so difficult to remember the plan they had come up with? Zia shook her head and softened her tone slightly. "I do not worry about Ivan or any of his men finding us this early in our journey. But I do think the ruse necessary. I have read much about highwaymen who roam the county roads, falling upon the carriages of the wealthy and important people. What if one should take us prisoner and try to ransom me?"

She checked her reflection in the mirror one last time before moving to the doorway. She looked as poor as she possibly could with her naturally regal nose and chin. "Come; our carriage will be waiting for us and we have yet to procure any food."

Tiana looked at her mistress skeptically. "But how will they know you," she looked down at the cloak, "or rather, *I*, am someone important enough to be ransomed?"

Zia raised her brows, her mouth set in a straight line. "How many people of common birth have a cloak such as that?"

Tiana frowned. "So I am to be the one held prisoner and ransomed? This is your plan?" Her voice rose slightly in pitch.

Zia let out an exasperated sigh. "Yes, of course. Is that not why you are here? To see to my needs? I need not be taken prisoner." Zia waved her hand at her maid. "It is only a precaution, Tiana. I do not think it truly a possibility." She glared at her maid, the full extent of the girl's question suddenly dawning. "You do not wish for *me* to be taken prisoner, do you?"

"Of course not, miss." At least she had not called Zia by her title again. But her voice held a touch too much uncertainty for Zia's liking.

Tiana fixed her hair and tied Zia's bonnet under her chin. "And you think they will believe I am someone important?" Her voice held a small hint of excitement.

Zia shrugged, turning the knob on the door. "By the time they figure out you are not, I shall be safely away." She turned back. "But not to worry. I should think I would come back for you."

Tiana did not look altogether reassured by the statement, but nonetheless, she turned away from the mirror and followed Zia from the room. "When did you tell your uncle we would be arriving?"

Zia waved her hand. She had not given her uncle a timeline. To do so, she would have had to write him, which she had not done. "I was not sure how long the journey would take, so I did not give him specifics." In truth, she had been afraid that notifying her uncle before their arrival would only give him a chance to send word to her father. While she was certain her uncle would dispatch that exact letter upon her arrival at Chatney House, she did not wish her father to have any advance notice.

Her sigh caught in her throat as she thought on Papa. She had been sad to leave him, but he had left her little choice with his ultimatums.

As she neared the bottom of the stairs, she could see into the common room of the inn. The innkeeper's wife bustled about, setting food out on the sideboard. She glanced up when Zia stepped to the floor and narrowed her eyes.

Zia took in a large breath, momentarily regretting the demanding tone she'd used the night before. But it had been very late, and she had been tired. Could the woman not understand such things?

Tiana walked over and gave the woman a smile. "Good morning. I am afraid we shall be taking our leave today."

Zia walked over and pulled Tiana away. "Forgive my mistress. She is not used to your English customs." Zia glared at her maid. They would never believe Tiana was a lady if she continually visited with the servants. "Would it be possible for us to collect some food to take with us? We are most anxious to get underway."

The older woman glared at them. "If it means bein' rid of ye sooner, I should gather the food myself."

Tiana smiled weakly. "Yes, I suppose you would." She leaned around Zia and pressed several coins into the woman's hand. "I apologize for any inconvenience we have been to you. We shall gather a few things and be on our way."

The woman sniffed and grunted. Turning, she pushed through a curtain separating the main room from the kitchens in the back.

Zia quietly moved to the buffet and picked up a serviette, placing bread and biscuits into her palm. She stood in front of the plate of ham, debating with herself the prudence in taking the meat. It would surely keep hunger at bay longer, but it was certain to make quite a mess of the serviette and anything else inside of it. Her stomach grumbled, effectively ending her hesitation. She speared two thick slices with a fork and placed them atop a slice of bread. She added a second piece of bread on top, hoping to eliminate some of the mess.

She glanced around her. The innkeeper's wife would certainly object to Zia taking this much food. Seeing no one paying her any mind, Zia snatched several boiled eggs and tucked them under the biscuits. She folded in the two sides of the serviette and tied the ends up before making a second package for Tiana.

Tiana waited quietly in a chair by the fireplace.

Zia turned in search of the footman and ran headlong into a gentleman waiting for his turn at the sideboard. His bearded mouth ticked up slightly.

Zia gave him a small push away. "Excuse me, sir. You need not stand so close. There will be food enough when I have departed."

The smile, however small it was, slipped and was replaced by a very evident frown. One brow was arched high on his forehead. The brow slowly lowered, and his eyes narrowed. "I beg your pardon, miss."

Zia sidestepped the man and moved to speak with the footman they had hired along with the carriage and driver.

Thomas dipped his head. "The trunks have been loaded into the carriage, miss. It is ready to leave when you are."

Zia glanced over her shoulder at Tiana and motioned her to the door. Zia closed her eyes briefly. It would be a relief when they were at last in the carriage. Tiana came and stood beside Zia. "Come, mistress. The carriage is ready."

Tiana nodded and moved toward the door. She smiled at the footman who colored up at the attention.

Zia gritted her teeth. It would take divine intervention to not have the whole of England know of their arrival. "Please quit flirting with the servants, *my lady*. You are drawing undue attention to us," she whispered fiercely.

Zia glanced over her shoulder to verify her assertion and saw the bearded man look her way. Was he suspicious of her? Could this be what a highwayman looked like? Not that this is what he would look like when he was *actually* robbing carriages. From what Zia had read, highwaymen usually wore cloth covers over their mouths to hide their identity. But still, this man looked dangerous.

"Hurry along, Tiana. We must be on our way."

"Did you see that man looking at you, *knyázhna?*"

Zia followed Tiana's gaze back to the man filling his plate with food.

"I did see him. I bumped into him after retrieving our breakfast. He must have been making sure I was not hurt." Zia motioned to the door with her head. "Now, let us hurry." She felt as if he still stared at her, but she did not dare look back and verify the truthfulness of it.

Tiana moved toward the door and their waiting carriage.

The wind nearly pulled the door from Zia's grasp. She tightened her hold and pushed it closed behind them. Her bonnet lifted, pulling at the ribbons tied beneath her chin. She hurried to the carriage and allowed Thomas to hand her in after Tiana. He shut the door and the two settled into the velvet covered cushions.

The carriage shifted as the wind pushed against it.

"Do you think it safe to travel in such conditions, Your Highness?"

Zia lifted a brow but made no comment. "It is not the most ideal weather, I concede. But I do not think it will lessen in the near future. We cannot put off our travels to my uncle's estate." She looked out the window. "Besides, the weather was much worse when we left Odessa. We shall be well." Zia's brow furrowed as she stared out the window. When they had left home, Boris had been driving the carriage. She trusted Boris with her life, but this man...Henry? She did not know of his skill in the driver's box.

Tiana must have sensed Zia's apprehension. "I hope so," she whispered.

The carriage lurched forward and both women sucked in a breath.

Zia slowly released hers as the carriage took on a steady rhythm. Taking one more deep breath, she settled into the seat, dropping her head against the side of the carriage and watching the landscape outside slide past her window. Snow began to fall, and she gave a slight shiver.

Tiana leaned forward, grasping the rug lying on the opposite seat. She unfolded it and draped it across Zia's lap. "I do not wish you to catch a cold." She moved one of the bricks from her own feet to Zia's.

Zia smiled. Perhaps she had been too terse with the girl earlier. While Zia was often irritated and cross with her maid, she was grateful Tiana was there.

Tiana was her reluctant traveling companion, but she was also her friend. Or as much of a friend as a servant could be to a princess. Indeed, she was the only friend Zia had ever had. They had practically grown up together.

Zia pulled the rug over, placing half of it onto Tiana's lap. "I should not like to see you become ill, either."

Tiana slid the blanket back onto Zia. "You forget, I am wearing your cloak. I find I am quite warm. But I know the cloak you are wearing cannot boast as much. Take the rug and wrap it around you, *knyázhna*."

Zia nodded and tucked the blanket around her legs and arms. Tiana was right; her cloak did not provide the warmth that Zia's heavy woolen one did. Why had Tiana never mentioned this before?

Turning her attention back out the window, Zia pushed those troubling thoughts from her mind. Perhaps when they reached her uncle's estate, she could see that Tiana had a warmer cloak made.

Her uncle. That thought brought a deep sigh. She had not actually met her mother's brother. From all accounts, the Duke of Heathrough was a stern man. But surely, he would take Zia in and protect her from Prince Sokolov. Indeed, Zia did not know what she would do if her uncle refused her. What if he sent her back? She swallowed past the tightness in her throat. She would not—could not—think on that now.

A hard wind hit the side of the carriage and it leaned heavily to Zia's side. She scooted away from the window, nearly hugging Tiana in the middle of the seat.

Tiana looked at her with slightly wide eyes. "Why do you look so concerned? I thought you said we would be safe here."

Zia shrugged. "Nothing has happened to make me think otherwise. I will feel better when we reach Chatney House, is all. My uncle will see we are safe."

Tiana narrowed her eyes slightly. Did she not believe Zia? The girl knew better than to voice that suspicion if she indeed thought it.

Zia pushed herself against the side of the carriage and leaned her head against the cold glass. Another gust shook them, and Zia could feel the wheels slipping beneath them. She sighed. More than just the weather was reminiscent of Russia. The hills outside her window reminded her of the hilly region outside Odessa.

The landscape dropped away in a valley below. Zia looked across the carriage out the other window and saw the carriage hugging tightly to the hillside. While it was not an immense drop on her side, it was enough to make her stomach clench. If the weather were not so disagreeable, this ride would have been quite lovely and enjoyable. But currently, it had Zia shifting slowly toward Tiana.

Another gust pushed against the carriage, this time shifting it closer to the hillside. Zia let out a relieved breath. Better that than the threatening cliffside on the opposite side of the road. The gust released its hold on them, and the carriage swerved, bringing them dangerously close to the edge. The front jerked back toward the hillside, but the back wheel must have caught the edge because the carriage slipped and leaned dangerously over the drop-off.

Tiana yelled out, as Zia pushed them both to the opposite side. But their body weight was not enough to bring the carriage into balance, and it tipped the rest of the way, landing on its side and sliding down the hillside.

Tiana screamed and fell on top of Zia, but her screams quieted as the carriage came to a hard stop. Tiana fell to the side, as Zia fell forward striking her head on the door latch. Blood trickled from Tiana's nose. Her eyes fluttered closed and then her body went limp.

"Tiana. Tiana." Zia screamed at her maid. "Wake up, Tiana. I insist you wake up." Zia looked up at the sky through the window in the door of the carriage. She shook the girl. "We must hurry. Perhaps there will be a passing carriage. But you must first wake up."

Tiana said nothing and made no movement. Zia yanked the glove from her hand and placed shaking fingers to the girl's throat. Perhaps she was not doing it right. She had only seen it done once by the doctor when her mother had died.

Zia moved her fingers along Tiana's throat. *Feel something.* She willed her fingers to find a heartbeat. "Fine. I shall get Thomas to come help me get you out."

Zia pushed up on the door and pulled herself out of the carriage. She looked around in the blowing snow. Where were Thomas and Henry? Surely they did not leave her and Tiana to save themselves. She put her hand at her brows, blocking the snow and wind from distorting her vision. "Thomas! Henry!" She screamed but the wind seemed to blow her words back into her face. She hollered several times to no avail. The men were nowhere to be found.

"I shall find a carriage myself." Zia climbed toward the road, her half boots slipping on the mud and snow. She fell and cursed herself for leaving her glove in the carriage. Not that her other hand was dry or warm.

Her head pounded and her chest burned as the cold air filled her lungs. Finally, muddy and soaked through, she reached the edge of the road. Her foot slipped again, and she landed hard. Zia dropped her head onto her arm, closing her eyes. She was so tired. Perhaps if she could rest for a moment... Pops of color filled the space behind her eyelids only to fade into a silent blackness.

CHAPTER 3

T hey had started out later than he had hoped and now they were in the thick of the storm. He would surely be late for his scheduled appointment with Lord Somerton. Dawson grunted as he watched the snow pound against the carriage window then glanced at his mother to assess if she was concerned.

There was less concern than curiosity.

"I can understand why that young lady was scared of you, Dugray. You look a fright with all that hair on your face. When I stepped off the boat and first saw your face, I had hoped to see all of it. Why have you not shaved?"

Dawson looked across the carriage at his mother. "I will see it is all shaved off once we arrive at Fawnbrooke, Mother. I did not feel it necessary to drag my valet on this adventure." Dawson stroked at his beard. "Besides, I believe it keeps me warmer."

His mother shook her head, her lips pursed in exasperation. "You look as if you are exploring the Louisiana Territory."

Dawson chuckled until the carriage pulled to a stop and he

looked out. The snow was coming down almost horizontal, the wind was so fierce. There was no town or even shelter within sight. Why had James stopped? "What is the matter, Son? You look worried?"

Dawson gave his mother's hand a reassuring pat. "I am sure there is nothing wrong, Mother. I am just unsure why the carriage has stopped."

As if answering his question, the door opened, flying out of the footman's hand and banging loudly against the side of the carriage. "Begging you pardon, sir."

Dawson leaned forward. "Why have we stopped, William?"

The footman squinted into the carriage. "It looks as if there has been an accident up ahead. A carriage has gone over the hillside."

Dawson swore.

His mother's eyes widened slightly, and he was not sure if it was because of the curse or the news of the accident. Regardless, he buttoned his greatcoat as he stepped from the carriage. "Stay inside where it is warm, Mother. I do not wish for you to catch cold."

She nodded.

Dawson held his hat on with his hand and trudged into the wind. The snow pelted against his face, like tiny daggers. He squinted, trying to keep the snow out of his eyes. What happened to the beautiful, lilting flakes from just a few days ago?

He walked to the edge and looked down, his mouth dropping open. A snowy, muddy trail went the whole length of the hillside, ending at the splinted carriage box at the bottom. Dawson surveyed the area, shaking his head. Where was the driver? And what of the occupants? Had they been thrown clear or were they still inside? He doubted anyone had survived.

"Sir." James jogged up to Dawson, hooking his thumb over his shoulder. "There seems to be a woman over there. She must have been trying to climb up the hillside and slipped."

Dawson looked to where the driver motioned. A mound, quickly being covered by snow, lay just up ahead. Dawson hurried over.

Her head and arms rested on the road's outer edge, but the rest of her hung limp down the hillside. "Is she alive?"

"I dunno." James shifted from foot to foot.

Dawson dropped down to one knee, feeling the mud oozing through his pants. He gently turned her over and she let out a soft moan. Dawson sat back on his haunches. It was the servant woman from the inn. The one who had bumped into him at the sideboard. Her face was pale and dotted with mud and snow.

"Help me pull her up." He called back to James and the two brought her up onto the road. "She is soaked through." Dawson dropped back to his knee and lifted her up into his arms. "There must be a driver somewhere down here. Please make a search while I situate her in the carriage with my mother."

"Surely you do not think there is anyone alive down there?" James placed his hand over his eyes. "Look at the carriage."

Dawson scowled. "She survived, did she not?"

"Perhaps she was thrown before the carriage went over." James peered down.

Dawson shook his head. "No. I could see her tracks in the mud. If there is someone else alive, they will not be for this world long if we do not hurry."

James and William grudgingly stepped off the road, their arms waving about as they slid nearly a rod.

Dawson hurried to the carriage and fumbled for the handle. His mother must have opened it from inside, because the door flung back on the wind, narrowly missing both him and the woman in his arms.

She let out a soft moan.

"You are going to be well," he whispered in her ear. *Or I hope you shall be.* The carriage shifted as he stepped up and ducked inside.

"Oh, dear me. Is she all right?" His mother looked on with worried eyes. "Is she...alive?"

"She is for now. But if we do not get her warm soon, I am not certain she will be for long."

James hollered up from the carriage below.

"Please get her some blankets, Mother." Dawson ducked back out of the carriage and returned to the edge of the road.

"We found the driver and the footman, sir. They are shaken, but they were able to jump clear before the carriage went over." He glanced over at the carriage. "But the lady inside..." James did not need to finish the sentence for Dawson to know of her fate.

"Come up, all of you. Let us get to the next village and then we can decide how to proceed." He glanced back at the carriage. "The lady needs to see a doctor. Or at the very least, gain some warmth and nourishment. I will also need to send word to Lord Somerton that I will not be coming as planned."

The men scurried up, slipping frequently in the mud. William handed a cloak over to Dawson. "I thought this might be helpful for the girl, sir."

Dawson clutched the furry cloak. "Thank you, William."

The drivers climbed into the box in the front while the two footmen squeezed into the tight space at the back.

Dawson looked down at his muddy boots and pants for the first time. "I hope Tad does not go apoplectic when he sees his carriage," he muttered. "But there is nothing for it." He hoisted himself back into the carriage, looking around to see where the mud would be the least noticeable. When he saw the lady's pale face, he forgot about everything else. Pulling his hand from his glove, he put it to her face. Her skin was cold to the touch. She needed warmth quickly.

He sat her up, dropping down on the bench next to her and draping the heavy cloak around her shoulders. Her lips held a tinge of purple, but her body shook, and her teeth clattered together, giving him hope she was well enough.

"She is freezing. Mother, are there any warm bricks left?"

His mother shook her head. "They gave up heat several hours ago, I am afraid."

Carefully he laid her head in his lap. Rubbing his hand up and down her arm, he tried to infuse some heat into her body. His wet glove left gooseflesh in its wake. He peeled it off and threw it to the floor next to its match.

"To the devil with propriety," he growled and pulled her onto his lap, pressing her body against his. He ignored the uptick in his pulse as he felt the slight tickle of her breath on his neck. He also ignored the slight raise of his mother's brow.

He tucked the cloak around her and then pulled his greatcoat over the both of them, wrapping his arms around her shivering body.

Her eyes fluttered open and she stared at him. He returned her stare until her eyes drifted closed again.

"She needs a doctor." His mother's voice was quiet and concerned.

Dawson nodded. "We are past the most dangerous part. We should be to a town within the hour. We can summon a doctor there." He looked out the window. "If he says she can travel, we should be able to make it home to Fawnbrooke tonight."

Dawson sucked in a breath. *Fawnbrooke. Home.* It was odd to use those two words together. Indeed, Dawson had only decided to buy the place just before setting out for Liverpool, after visiting the estate nearly half a dozen times. Tad had volunteered to make the necessary arrangements while Dawson was away. He now hoped he had not made a rash decision that would end poorly.

The carriage turned from the road and proceeded up the gravel drive. Dawson partially relaxed. Their brief consultation with a doctor had indicated it would be best to get the woman home and into a warm bed as quickly as possible. Sleep is what she needed. The innkeeper where they'd stopped had seemed none too thrilled with the prospect of caring for the stranger and so Dawson felt he had little option but to keep her with him. Though he hadn't caused the accident, he somehow felt responsible for the woman; after all, someone would have to tell her the news of her mistress's passing. Even the hired driver and footman had stayed behind at the inn, claiming no personal connection to the traveling women, and clearly anxious to be done with their ill-fated journey. The woman was utterly alone. As soon as the weather broke, Dawson had taken her and his mother and set out for Fawnbrooke.

He looked down at the woman in his lap and his stomach gave a little lurch. She had not awakened at all since her eyes had fluttered open just after her rescue, but her body was warming, and a little color had returned to her cheeks. His mother had told him she thought it not necessary for the girl to continue on his lap, but he had disputed. What if she should roll off the bench and injure herself further? No, he would see her safely to Fawnbrooke. It was the least he could do.

The carriage slowed and Dawson looked out the window. Fawnbrooke sat outlined in the moonlight breaking through the clouds. It was even more beautiful than he remembered. Perhaps it was because it was night. Or maybe it was because it was his. Whatever the reason, he was glad to be at the end of their journey.

The carriage came to a stop. His mother looked at him wearily. "Are we here?"

Dawson nodded, his stomach jittery for another reason. What if his mother did not like Fawnbrooke? What if she was disappointed in it—in him? "The house is in need of repairs. I hope you are not disappointed."

His mother smiled. Oh, he had missed her. She always seemed able to set him at ease. "It is a roof over head; if it does not sway to the waves, then I shall be quite content."

Dawson placed one arm behind the lady's back and the other beneath her legs. He scooped her into his arms and ducked his head as he stepped from the carriage.

A small tendril of smoke curled from the chimneys in the east wing. Dawson smiled. *Thank you, Tad.* When he had sent word they were coming early, he had not anticipated this.

William pushed open the front door and Dawson turned sideways as he shuffled into the house. He paused as he looked around the entryway. It looked different than last he saw it. The floors were polished to a shine, as were the side tables, holding vases of hothouse flowers, lining the entryway walls. The walls had not been painted, but the plaster was patched, and the wallpaper had been removed.

His mother stepped in behind him. "Oh, Dugray. It is lovely, Son."

Dawson swallowed. "I must thank Tad when next I see him. This is all his doing." What had he done in his life to deserve a friend like Tad?

Mrs. Bryse, the cook from Morley Park, shuffled out of the kitchen. "Ah, Mr. Dawson, sir. You are back."

Dawson looked on the woman with creased brows. "Mrs. Bryse, what are you doing here? It is much too late for you to be awake, much less away from home."

She smiled and waved him aside. "When your missive arrived indicating your change in plans, Her Grace was determined you would not return to a cold, empty house, with no food at all." She grimaced. "It is not much, but there is some soup warming in the pot on the stove and a loaf of bread on the table. I will see that some breakfast is brought over in the morning."

Dawson shook his head. "No, you are too kind, but I cannot accept it."

Mrs. Bryse patted his arm. "Her Grace insisted on it." She looked at the woman in his arms. "Besides, you seem to have your arms full already."

She waved William over. "It is only until you are able to hire your own staff, sir." She turned to William. "I am sure Mr. Dawson would appreciate you taking the woman to her room." She pulled on her bonnet and pelisse, her brow creased. "All the rooms have been dusted and aired out. Three of the rooms have proper beds made up."

Dawson shook his head, trying to process everything that had happened in the last few hours. "Yes, there was a carriage accident on the hillside road." He had said as much in the missive, but for some reason, he felt compelled to mention it again.

William came to take the woman, but Dawson shook his head, unwilling to relinquish her yet. It would only be a moment more until he would have to leave her in her chambers and then he would be unable to see her until she was recovered.

Mrs. Bryse raised a hand to her mouth. "That is just terrible, sir." She placed a hand on the lady's face. "The poor dear." Her lips pursed. "She will need more than a little breakfast sent over tomorrow. I shall send Alice over right away. She is my most capable assistant."

Dawson knew he should decline the offer, but he was at a loss to do so. "Thank you, Mrs. Bryse."

"Nonsense, sir." She gave one last tug on the bow beneath her chin and moved toward the door. "Is James still outside?"

Dawson nodded. The woman in his arms felt heavy and the exertion of the rescue was catching up with him. He took a few steps back, leaning his tired body against the wall.

"I'll send Alice back with James," Mrs. Bryse yelled over her shoulder as she disappeared through the door.

"She is right, Son. The girl needs to be in bed."

Dawson nodded reluctantly and moved toward the staircase. "Now, if you will accompany me. She has become quite heavy."

They moved up the stairs and to the first empty room with a bed. Dawson carefully placed her on the mattress before his mother shooed him toward the door. "I will take care of her now. You go on."

Dawson nodded and left the room. He stopped in the corridor and looked around. This was home. He let the thought settle on him, a smile spreading across his face. Yes, now that his mother was here, this place felt like home.

CHAPTER 4

"Y̲ou will be well." The voice floated about in Zia's brain with a pair of dark brown eyes set amongst a great deal of hair. Why was a bear haunting her dreams?

A low moan sounded, penetrating Zia's thoughts. Where was it coming from? Tiana must be having a fitful dream again.

Zia snuggled down into the soft covers, not wishing to emerge from the warmth and comfort of her current situation. Another moan sounded, and only then did she realize the sound was coming from her mouth. Zia curled her legs up and her muscles pulsed in pain. What had she done to tax them so?

She took a deep breath and cracked an eye open, pushing herself up in alarm when she recognized none of her surroundings. This was not her room. No silk curtain hung beside the bed.

The walls were patched in many places and were in need of paint. The furniture looked well used. Zia searched the room for Tiana. Was she getting Zia a tray? Zia pressed herself against the headboard. "Tiana?" Her voice was barely a whisper. She closed her mouth and cleared the dryness from her throat. "Tiana," she yelled with slightly more pitch and volume.

The door opened and Zia relaxed until she saw an older woman enter the room.

"You have awakened at last. I have brought you some tea." She placed the tray on the side table. "I thought you might be hungry, so I also have some bread and cheese." Her voice was kind and soft, as was her face, but Zia was still on her guard.

"Where is Tiana?"

The woman's brow furrowed. "Tiana?"

Zia scooted to the far side of the bed and drew the covers up to her chin. "Yes, my maid. Where is she?"

The woman shook her head. "I am sorry. I do not know to whom you are referring. We only found you and the lady you were with."

Zia gave a snort and relaxed. Tiana must still be acting out the charade they had planned upon arriving in England. "Would you please ask her to come to me? And tell her to bring the green dress. I shall wear it today to meet my uncle. We are close to Chatney House, are we not?"

The woman's brow creased deeper the more Zia talked. "I am sorry, but you were the only one inside the carriage to survive, miss. Even your trunks and their contents were completely destroyed. There was only that night gown and one dress—which I was able to mend— that were not ripped asunder. Everything else..." she trailed off and bit her lower lip.

"What do you mean I was the only one to survive? And what happened to my trunks?" Zia would ring peal over Tiana's head for this one.

"Do you not remember the accident?" The woman turned her back to Zia and began to pour tea into the cup. She turned back and held out the cup. "Your carriage overturned and slipped down the hillside on the way here. The Lady in the carriage with you perished. Your driver and footman were not injured. We have paid them their wages and sent them on their way." The woman took a seat next to the bed, her hands clasped in her lap. "It was providential we arrived when we did, for I do not think you would have lasted much longer out in the cold."

Zia shook her head. Accident? There had been an accident, and Tiana was dead? Closing her eyes, Zia tried to remember. Vague images of their hired carriage lurching on the road and then the feel of Tiana's heavy body upon her floated into her mind. It felt like a dream. Should not something so terrible crash into your thoughts like the tragedy it was?

Zia fought against the panic rising in her chest. The teacup rattled in her hands. No. This could not be happening. What would she do without Tiana? She had been with Zia since childhood. How could Zia go on to her uncle's without Tiana?

The woman gently took the cup and returned it to the tray before turning sympathetic eyes on Zia.

Zia's breaths came out in quick, jerky gulps. This was not how she had planned this journey. What was she to do now? She readjusted herself in the bed, and again her muscles ached in protest. It seemed for now, she was to stay right here. But where exactly was here? She lifted slightly wide eyes to the woman. "Who are you and where am I, exactly?"

The woman smiled. She did that often. Was it a nervous reaction or was she genuine? In Zia's experience, it must be the former. Few people of her acquaintance were naturally kind, not without some motive behind their generosity. Although, Zia conceded, her mother had been kind. So perhaps this woman was in earnest.

"I am Mrs. Dawson and you are at my son's estate, Fawnbrooke. It is just outside the village of Shearsby in Leicestershire."

Zia noted the pride in the woman's voice. She looked around

and let out a small snort. What was there to be proud of in this place? While there were no actual holes in the walls any longer, Zia was certain that could not be true of all the rooms, unless they had put her in the worst one in the house, which seemed unlikely, as she was a guest. "This is what you call an estate in England? I should wonder at what you call the places where your poor live."

The woman's smile dropped, and she moved back to the tray, retrieving the plate of bread and cheese. "Yes, well, he has only just bought the place. He is to fix it up; I dare say, when he is done, it will rival any great house of your acquaintance."

Zia looked away, already missing Tiana and her soothing way. The woman seemed affronted by Zia's honest appraisal. Well, let her be offended. They had encountered a few inns in such disrepair, but Zia had insisted they find different accommodations. Most of the time, it had been possible. She was not used to staying in such conditions for an extended period of time. No princess would ever consider it.

She cleared her throat. "I really must write to my uncle and inform him of my situation. I am sure he could come and fetch me." She moved to get out of the bed, but the gentle hand on her arm stopped her.

"You are not well enough to leave your bed. Of that, I am certain." She pushed Zia back onto the pillows behind her and tucked the bed covers around her. "I shall bring you some paper and ink once you have finished eating."

Zia opened her mouth to protest but was effectively cut off.

"You have been asleep for nearly two days. I am sure you are hungry. Your letter can wait a few hours more. I will take it to the village in the morning and post it for you, if you so desire." She brought the tray over and placed it on Zia's lap. "For now, eat. Your body needs to heal."

Zia nodded dutifully and took a bite of her bread. She closed her eyes, realizing for the first time how hungry she truly was. She had not tasted bread this delicious in weeks. Not since leaving home.

She chewed quietly, her mind turning over all the information she had learned. Her emotions were a jumble. She ached at the loss of Tiana. There were many people who claimed a friendship when it was to their advantage, but only Tiana had been there when Zia needed her. They had grown up together on Zia's father's estate. What would she tell Tiana's mother?

In truth, this was all Zia's fault. Tiana had not thought this trip a prudent idea, but Zia had insisted she was leaving Odessa with, or without Tiana. In the end, Tiana had acquiesced and had come along. And now she was dead.

Who would protect Zia now?

"When you feel up to it, you are welcome to join me downstairs. But I would advise waiting a few days, at least." Mrs. Dawson frowned slightly. "I am certain it will not be up to your standards. But you are welcome, none the less." She turned toward the door. "I shall be in the North Parlor. Lucy can come and fetch me if you are in need of me." She gave one last nod and walked, chin raised, from the room.

Zia sighed. What had she gotten herself into? She finished the cheese and bread, wishing there were several more slices of each, and drank the last of her tea.

She lifted the tray from her lap and set it aside. Pushing the covers off her legs, she swung them over the side and placed them on the floor. Slowly she rose, testing her legs before putting all her weight on them. They ached but seemed able to hold her well enough.

She walked over to the window and looked outside. The sky was gray, and a thin layer of snow covered the earth below her. A shiver shook her whole body and gooseflesh roughened her skin.

Even now she could be out in the cold, buried in a carriage coffin, if not for these people. She shut her eyes and wrapped her arms around her middle.

Perhaps she would be better placed to keep her less than complimentary comments to herself for the time being. She was warm and now fed. Her heart sank. It was more than Tiana could boast.

She was grateful at least the driver and footman had not been injured. Although, she did not believe they should have accepted their pay. After all, it was Henry's fault the carriage had gone over. She should pay Mrs. Dawson and her son back the money they had paid the servants.

Zia looked around the room, but her reticule was nowhere in sight. She rushed to the wardrobe and yanked open the doors. Just as Mrs. Dawson had said, only one dress hung on the rack along with her cloak. The cloak Tiana had been wearing. On the floor below it, Zia found her reticule.

She snatched the small bag up and slammed the door closed on the wardrobe, and the memories. She held her reticule to her chest, the action helping to calm her racing heart. What would she have done if it had been lost? She would have lost all her money, the miniature of her mother, and the ring her father had given her. She had lost enough without losing this as well. She pulled the ribbon handle over her arm and returned to the bed, suddenly too fatigued to stand.

Zia kept to her room for the next few days. Mrs. Dawson came to check on her each morning, but her smile was not as forthcoming as it had been that first day.

Zia sat often at her window and stared at the church yard a

short distance off, the single heap of freshly turned dirt holding Zia's complete attention. She knew at some point she would have to go down and face the grave—face the part she played in Tiana's death. She stood up, her muscles aching less than they had the day before. She pressed a hand against her stomach. Perhaps she still was not well enough to see Tiana.

A knock sounded at the door and Lucy peeked her head in. "Ah, miss. You are up and about. Mrs. Dawson said to inform you that you were welcome to join her in the parlor. I believe she is in need of company."

Zia started to shake her head, but then her gaze flicked out the window. Suddenly, she needed out of this room—needed to be away from the hold the view of the churchyard seemed to have over her. She needed company.

Zia nodded. "Could you help me dress? I find I am tired of staring at these same four walls."

The girl nodded, but Zia did not miss the puzzled look on her face as she went to the wardrobe to fetch a dress. What was that about? It was obvious the girl was not a lady's maid, but surely, she knew how to fasten buttons.

"How long have you worked here, Lucy?"

The girl looked over her shoulder at Zia. "Just a few days, miss. I was a 'tween maid at Morley Park. Mrs. Bryse thought I might be able to make a better go of it if I came here to Fawnbrooke early on, before the house is in need of more servants."

Zia smiled, trying to put the girl at ease. "It seems a fortunate situation, indeed." The words came out a little stilted—Zia was not used to making idle conversation with the servants—but surely Lucy did not notice.

The maid returned with a pale lavender dress in her arms. Zia shook her head. "No. I am guessing you have never served as a lady's maid before, but that is a walking gown, not a morning dress."

The girl's brow furrowed. "But miss, it is the only dress in the wardrobe."

Zia's shoulders fell. "Oh, yes. I had forgotten about my trunks." She paused, momentarily lamenting the loss of her wardrobe. "Then I suppose I have little choice in the matter."

Lucy waited patiently as it seemed to take an excruciating amount of time for Zia to move each muscle group. Just raising her arms over her head to remove her night gown seemed to tax her to her limit. Zia's breath caught in her throat when she caught sight of her body in the mirror. Several greenish-yellow bruises ran the length of her torso.

Her eyes lifted. The bruise running the length of her cheek had only slightly faded. It would likely be a week or more before the bruises went away. In truth, there was barely a place to set her hand on her thighs or torso without touching a scrape or discolored patch of skin.

Zia swallowed hard.

"Come, miss. I am sure you are cold. Let us finish getting you dressed."

Zia nodded, but her eyes never left the reflection in the mirror. If this was what she looked like, she could not imagine poor Tiana. Her eyes closed as Lucy pulled the chemise and then the gown over Zia's head. The cool softness of the fabric felt good against her skin. It was pleasant to be in something other than her nightgown.

Zia moved to the dressing table and sat down. "I think a simple knot at the back will suffice for today, Lucy. It is not as if I am needing to impress anyone. I dare say this bruise will keep that from happening for quite some time."

"Oh, nonsense, miss. I am sure anyone of worth will see beyond the bruises." Lucy caught her gaze in the mirror.

Zia lifted a hand to her cheek, running her fingers down the bruise and the cut that ran from her hairline. Her face would never look the same. She was now marred. Her chin quivered and her eyes blurred. Would her uncle still grant her permission to live with him? It was not likely she would be the object of many suitors now.

She brushed the back of her hand across her eyes. No, now she would be the object of fortune hunters. But was that not what Prince Sokolov was? Did she really think she would do better than him in her current state?

Lucy tugged on her hair, wrapping it around itself until a tight chignon sat at the back of Zia's head. Pins poked her scalp, forcing tears to spill from her eyes.

The maid stepped back. "Anything else I can do for you, miss?" She seemed to emphasis the word *miss*. Why did she do that? Was it an English pronunciation or was there something else behind it?

Zia raised her hand to her hair. "No. I am well, Lucy. That is all."

The girl curtsied, her brow raised, then quit the room.

I am well. Zia repeated the words in her mind. *I am well.* Was she really? She ran her fingers over the wound on her cheek again. The words felt hollow, much like she did. Would she ever really be well again?

CHAPTER 5

Dawson slammed the cover closed on the ledger and tossed his spectacles on top. He ran his hands through his hair and down his cleanly shaven face. He missed his beard. Especially when he went out of doors. But his mother seemed happier to see his whole face.

"Why did I let you talk me into this?" He scowled at Tad from across his desk.

"I do not see what you are growling about. Yes, it will be tight until the first crop comes in and even until the first horses are sold. But that is nothing. Look around you, Dawson. You own some of the best land in Leicestershire. How can you regret that?"

"I will regret it when the bank comes knocking and takes it all away. It will be another story of a son following in the footsteps of his father." He crossed his arms and lay them on his desk, dropping his head on top. "You always make things seem possible."

"This is not *im*possible. We will just need to be..." Tad steepled his fingers in front of his chin. "Judicious with your money."

Dawson raised his head and looked at his friend. "Oh, is that all? It seems all is to be well then." His scowl deepened. "How are we to mend the cottages with all this blasted snow? There is not enough to make fun with it, only to make things cold and slippery."

Tad nodded. "The weather does not seem to be working in our favor, does it?" He pursed his mouth to the side, thinking. "But it cannot stay like this for long. It never does."

Dawson gave Tad a bland look. "Says the man who has only lived here for two years."

Tad grinned. "My father shared many stories of his homeland. I believe I can make such a statement with confidence when I put both his knowledge and mine together."

Dawson heaved a heavy sigh. "What are we to do until the weather cooperates? I do not dare begin repairs on the main house until the cottages are done and ready to let."

Tad stared out the window behind Dawson. "You have gathered the materials for the cottages?"

Dawson nodded. "Yes, they are being stored in the barn. I had considered storing them in the cottages themselves, so as not to have to move them again. But with this burst of cold weather and the cottages so far removed from my view, I was afraid the materials may disappear if left within."

"You see? You are already thinking like a landowner."

Dawson stared hard at Tad. How did his friend maintain such an attitude? He had always been optimistic about the future. The only time Dawson had ever seen him dejected or hopeless was just after his father had died, and when Violet had been kidnapped and taken to Gretna Green. It was a trait Dawson envied, as he was Tad's complete opposite.

"You did not answer my question. What are we to do until we can mend the cottages?"

Tad shrugged. "I suppose there is little to do but wait it out." He put his fingers back to his chin. "Has the maid you rescued awakened yet?"

Dawson nodded. "Yes, but she keeps to her chambers."

"Have you discovered who she is?"

Dawson again shook his head. "No. If there were any papers to indicate such things, they were lost in the crash. I am afraid until she emerges, we will have no answers."

Tad pushed himself from the chair and rolled his shoulders. "I do hope, come spring, you can at least purchase a more comfortable chair for your guests. This one is dreadfully uncomfortable."

Dawson raised a brow at him. "Perhaps it is all part of my plan to get you to visit less."

Tad laughed. "What would you do with yourself without my daily visits? Besides, do I not find you at Morley Park just as often as I am here?"

"It is only because I cannot leave you without a secretary. Until you find a replacement, I feel it my duty to perform the task." It was not true and both men knew it. Indeed, Dawson did not know where life would have taken him if it were not for Tad and his family—Dawson's family. For he looked on them in quite the same way as he did his own. While he had no sisters, he knew he would do anything to protect Ainsley and Sarah just as Tad would.

The duke moved toward the door. "Yes, I am sure that is the reason." He placed his hand on the knob and turned back slightly. "I am off, but not before I see your mother. Is she about? I confess, having her here has both increased and lessened my desire to see my own mother again. How is that possible?"

Dawson allowed his lips to turn up ever so slightly. "I have no notion. But then, I am often at a lack to explain you, Your Grace."

Tad chuckled and Dawson moved past him into the corridor.

"Last I saw, Mother was at breakfast. I would guess she is in the North Parlor now. It is her favorite room in the house." He did not know why, as it was the room in need of the most repairs. He was sure it had been quite lovely in its day, but now the wallpaper hung limply in ripped patches and the plaster was cracked and missing in places. Just thinking on it made Dawson run a hand through his hair. What had he gotten himself into?

Dawson led Tad toward the parlor. He pushed through the door, his eyes immediately moving to his mother's favorite window seat. He frowned when she was not there. His gaze traveled around the room. The smell of gardenia hung in the air, which made him believe she had to be there somewhere.

His face relaxed when he saw her sitting on the settee in front of the fireplace. It was colder today; it should not have surprised him to find her there.

Dawson moved over to the settee and his mother raised her eyes to him, a small smile on her lips.

"Good morning, Mother."

Her smile widened when her eyes settled on Tad standing only a few steps behind. He sidestepped Dawson and planted a kiss on the woman's cheek. "It is good to see you, Mother D, even if only for a moment. I am back to Morley. Violet wishes to discuss a ball or some such nonsense." He sighed.

Dawson's mother patted his cheek. "And I know you will do so with a smile because you love her, and it will make her happy."

Tad grinned. "You know me too well."

The door creaked on its hinges and they all turned to see the servant girl from the carriage crash lurking in the doorway.

Dawson's pulse hammered in his throat. She was even more handsome than he remembered. And that was saying a great deal.

Her eyes looked about the room with a mixture of what seemed to be anxiousness and disdain, although which took prece-

39

dence he could not tell. Was she nervous about being at Fawn-brooke or was she just displeased with what she saw? Why should it bother him that she disapproved? He hardly knew her.

He turned to face his guest full on. "I see you have awakened. Welcome to Fawnbrooke, Miss—" There were a dozen or more questions he wanted to ask, but he refrained, not wishing to overwhelm the poor girl.

"*Princess* Zia Petrovich." She looked around the room and Dawson could not help but notice the slight upturn of her nose. What he did not notice was an accent. Curious. The Lady at the inn had definitely had an accent. "Thank you for taking me in. I suppose this is better than freezing."

With one sentence, the woman managed to set his heart to a normal rhythm.

His mother's mouth dropped open slightly and her eyes flicked to Dawson. Tad sucked in a deep breath behind him.

Princess? Did she really expect Dawson to believe she was a royal princess? Did he appear to be daft or easily canoodled? He looked her over, assessing her ilk. Nothing about her screamed royalty to him, save that blasted upturned nose. She did carry herself like a woman of gentle breeding. But still, a princess? His brow furrowed.

While Miss Petrovich surely had not made the connection, Dawson was certain this was the same girl he had seen at the inn. It was more likely the woman who had died in the carriage was the princess and this companion, or even simply her maid, was trying to improve her station now that no one could dispute her claim.

Dawson leveled his gaze at her. "Where are you from, *Princess?*"

Her chin rose at the insinuation in his tone.

"Odessa."

Dawson gave her a blank stare. He knew where Odessa was,

but he felt no inclination to acknowledge as much. At least not right away. His stare seemed to unnerve her slightly, and, he admitted, it felt good to feel even a small sense of control in the conversation.

"It is in Russia."

Dawson nodded. "Yes, I am aware. I do not detect much of an accent."

Miss Petrovich shrugged. "I learned English from my mother. She was raised in Derbyshire."

"And what brings a *princess* from Odessa to Leicestershire?" Dawson clasped his hands behind his back.

She ran her hands down the front of her gown, obviously trying to calm her nerves. Swallowing hard, she looked at the floor. "I ran away from Odessa. My father wished me to marry a most dreadful man."

Dawson frowned. "That still begs the question, why Leicestershire?"

"We were only passing through, Tiana and I." She paused and licked her lips several times, finally settling on biting her lower lip.

Dawson felt a slight tightening of his chest. The girl seemed to be genuinely in distress.

She returned her gaze to his. "We were on our way to my uncle's estate in Derbyshire. But the roads here are very ill maintained and our carriage slipped from the road."

"Your uncle lives in Derbyshire? Pray, who is he? The King of England?" Dawson did not mean to speak with such disdain, but he found himself hard pressed to restrain himself.

She stiffened and he felt a twinge of guilt. He did not know this woman and yet he felt compelled to confront her with her lies.

"No, in point of fact, he is the Duke of Heathrough."

Tad stepped forward. "The Duke of Heathrough is your uncle?"

She raised a brow. "And who is asking?"

Dawson took a step to the side and motioned to Tad. "*Princess* Zia Petrovich may I present, His Grace, the Duke of Shearsby."

A shadow of something, doubt perhaps, passed over her eyes. Was she regretting telling such lies now that she knew they would surely catch her?

"Do you know of my uncle?" There was hesitation in her voice.

Tad nodded. "Indeed. We have worked together on several bills in Lords. He squinted at her. "Come to think on it, he did mention once that his sister was married to a Russian Prince. I assume that to be your mother?"

Zia nodded slowly.

Dawson smiled. She was trapped and he was much looking forward to witnessing how she got out of these briars.

"My mother died several years ago."

Tad bowed to her. "I am sorry to hear of it. I know what it is like to lose a parent. How long are you to stay in England?"

Dawson stared at his friend. What was he doing? This woman did not deserve their kindness. She had taken his hospitality and now could do nothing but tell one bouncer after another.

The princess licked her lips again. "The duration of my stay will depend upon my uncle."

Tad nodded. "You are looking to him for refuge?" He grimaced. "I should like to see that conversation. As you are surely aware, your uncle is very conscious of propriety and duty."

Her already pale face seemed to blanch even more. "You do not believe he will protect me?"

Tad shrugged. "I cannot say for sure, but the man I know—" He left the rest of the sentence hanging in the air. He turned to Dawson and patted him on the back. "I should be on my way. I am sure Violet is likely on her way here as we speak." He placed another quick kiss on Dawson's mother's cheek. "I shall be eagerly awaiting further details," he mumbled as he passed in front of Dawson. He paused at the door, raising his voice as if for effect. "I will see you this afternoon." And with that, he left.

Dawson stared after Tad for a moment, trying to regain his thoughts. Turning back, he motioned for—what should he call her? It seemed odd to constantly refer to her as princess. Miss Petrovich? That seemed as good as anything. He motioned her over to the fainting couch and then took the chair opposite.

Once the lady was seated, he leaned forward. "I am sure you are anxious to get word to your uncle of your whereabouts."

Miss Petrovich nodded. "Yes. Your mother was kind enough to provide me with quill and ink when I first awakened."

Dawson grinned, but he knew it came across as more of a smirk. "Ah. Then you have already written. I am sure someone will be journeying into the village in the next few days and could post the letter for you, *Princess*."

She narrowed her eyes at him. "You need not use that tone, sir. I am not accustomed to such inferences." She fingered the trim on the settee cushion. "Thank you for what you did for Tiana." Her voice hitched a bit and Dawson felt the tightness in his chest again. Was she truly pained at the loss of her mistress or was this all an act to gain sympathy?

"I arranged with the vicar here at St. Peter's for her burial. She is in the churchyard."

She nodded. "Yes, I can see it from my chamber window." Her voice dropped to barely a whisper.

His chest had barely relaxed when it squeezed again. Dawson frowned. What was wrong with him? He had never let a woman do such things to him. He placed a hand over his heart and pushed, trying to release the pressure. It must have been something he had eaten which was causing this discomfort. The thought allowed him to take a deep breath.

He stared at her as she rubbed at the trim on the cushion beneath her. When first he had seen her, he had thought her rather pretty, but learning of her inclination toward untruths had dimmed her beauty somewhat.

He picked up his book which lay on the table next to his chair and turned to the page with the silken ribbon marking the location. He continued to glance up at her, studying her. What might have happened had she started their association with the truth? Could some sort of affection have developed between them? He shook his head. It did not matter what could have been, only what was, and what she was, *was* a liar.

CHAPTER 6

Zia fidgeted with the trim of the cushion beneath her. What was she doing? *She* did not fidget. She caused *others* to fidget. She glanced up at the man across from her. Something about him felt familiar, but she could not place it. Looking at his house, he should not elicit such a response from her.

She looked at the peeling paper and paint, the chipped and missing plaster. This man could not be someone of consequence. She squinted at him. But how did one of no station become friends with a duke? Her brow creased. This Mr. Dawson must have some standing in society, whether his house reflected that standing or not.

The muscles in her stomach tightened as she replayed the interaction between herself and Mr. Dawson in her mind. Her mouth pulled downward. Why had he said her title in such a way? It was as if he did not believe she was a princess. But why? Why should he not believe her? He did not know her. He did not know if she had a propensity to tell untruths. Why should the man assume so early in their acquaintance that she was a liar when she had been nothing but truthful? She crossed her arms across her chest, the rigidness of her body only increasing.

"What is wrong, Prin—" Mrs. Dawson looked at Zia, her brows crinkled in concern. Even this woman, who thus far had been kind to her, did not seem to believe her story.

Or perhaps she just did not know how to behave around royalty. Perhaps it would be better for them all if Zia did not dwell on her title. It did not seem to be doing her any favors of late.

"Please, call me Lady Zia."

Mr. Dawson snorted, and Zia narrowed her eyes at him.

Mrs. Dawson cleared her throat and the gentleman looked away. At least his mother knew how to get the man to behave properly.

She smiled at Zia. "Very well, my lady." She put her stitchery to the side and offered Zia her complete attention, placing a hand on her arm. "You seem troubled. I cannot say I would feel differently if I had awakened to learn what you have, but I am glad you have finally decided to leave your rooms."

Zia took long, deep breath. How did one voice all that she was feeling? Tiana was gone. She dropped her crossed arms to her middle, hugging herself. Her ears filled with noise, much like the time she had gone swimming in the pond on her father's estate.

Not only was Tiana gone, but now it seemed her uncle would very likely not welcome her into his household. How had her plans gone so terribly awry?

Mrs. Dawson placed a gentle hand on Zia's arm. "You are only looking more troubled. Is there nothing I can do to help you? Perhaps you left your bed too soon?"

Zia tried to swallow, but she felt as though she had cotton lodged in her throat. She forced a breath through her nose. "There is likely to be no reward for my safe return."

Mrs. Dawson's face only reflected confusion.

"I can assume that is the reason you are being nice to me—to ensure you get a reward from my father?"

Mrs. Dawson shook her head, but not before something flashed in her eyes. It looked to be hurt, or perhaps it was anger. Zia was not sure. It was not her usual custom to pay such close attention to those of a station so beneath her.

Mr. Dawson shot to his feet and Zia sat back with a jerk.

"You were in need of rescue, *Your Highness*." His voice was terse and clipped. "*That* is why we are being kind. Believe me when I say that I had no expectation of a reward." He eyed the walking dress Zia wore. "If I thought one would be offered for you."

Zia scooted into the corner of the settee, her frown returning. Mr. Dawson sounded angry, as if she had said something wrong. She was not accustomed to such emotions being tossed at her, except perhaps from her father and Prince Sokolov.

Mr. Dawson placed his hands behind his back and scowled down at her. "Perhaps now would be the time for you to write your father as well as your uncle. I should think he will be concerned over your location."

Mrs. Dawson picked up her sampler and began to stitch. "If the weather permits, I shall be going to the village tomorrow. I would be happy to post the letters for you."

So you may be rid of me all the quicker. The woman did not say as much in words, but her tone and demeanor said it for her.

Zia let out a frustrated breath. She'd had high hopes for her morning with Mrs. Dawson. How had it deteriorated so quickly? It was not likely that Mr. Dawson and his mother entertained people of quality, such as Zia, often, if ever. Perhaps they just did not understand how one was to treat a princess.

Granted, the Duke of Shearsby seemed to be on friendly terms with Mr. Dawson, but was that strictly because they were neighbors?

Perhaps Zia could find good company at the duke's estate, as Mrs. Dawson seemed less amiable than she had earlier.

"Thank you. I will hope for clear skies." Zia waited for the woman to stand and offer the proper curtsy before Zia left the room, but when Mrs. Dawson remained seated and did not so much as look in her direction, she slipped from the room without another word.

Zia walked down the corridor. While it did not seem as badly in need of repair as the room she had just left, it appeared the entire house was lacking. What kind of a gentleman was this Mr. Dawson?

She moved toward the stairs. Perhaps Mr. Dawson was right; she should begin her letter to her uncle now that she was feeling better, especially since she had implied she had done so already. But she could not seem to clear her head of what the duke had said about her uncle. While he had not come out directly and said the Duke of Heathrough would not help her, he did not seem to be convinced of the notion himself. What was she to do? If she sent a letter to her uncle and he did not wish to take her in, she had no place else to go. Worse, what if he wrote to her father and demanded she return to Odessa?

She turned instinctively to seek courage from Tiana, but the girl was not there. Zia closed her eyes. She could not lose herself to her worry, not when her safety in England depended on her uncle, and now, the Dawsons. She had to keep a clear head. What she needed was something to take her mind off of Tiana and the loneliness threatening to consume her, even just for a few hours.

As Zia wandered down the corridor, she peeked inside each room. There had to be a library in the house, did there not? At last, the second room from the end seemed promising. She stepped inside, instantly noticing the empty shelves that lined the perimeter of the room.

Zia's shoulders drooped. How was she to endure without even a book to read? She lamented the loss of her father's extensive library back in Odessa.

"May I help you find something?" Mr. Dawson's voice seemed to fill the room, as his body did the doorway, with irritation and displeasure.

Zia turned slowly toward the door, her head shaking. "I was only looking for a book to read." She almost apologized, as she would have to her father, for disturbing him. But she caught herself, instead raising her chin in challenge, also something she had been doing to her father of late.

Mr. Dawson let out something like a grunt or a growl. It was difficult to say precisely which sound it was. "I keep my books in my study. I have not had the time nor the inclination to stock the library shelves as of yet." He turned into the corridor but stopped after only a few steps and turned his head back, staring expectantly at Zia. "Do you wish to get a book or not?"

She nodded and hurried forward.

"Then follow me." He walked across the corridor and pushed through the door on the other side.

Zia followed behind, taking in the room. A large desk sat perpendicular to the large window on the back wall, giving Mr. Dawson a splendid view of the estate. Additionally, it put him in a similar situation to the door, making it so his back would never be to it. While the paper on the walls and the paint had not been repaired, the room still held a masculinity to it, although what gave that impression, she could not say. Perhaps it was simply because it smelled of Mr. Dawson. Earthy and masculine. She frowned. When had she taken notice of the man's scent?

He brushed past her and the smell of sandalwood and mint trailed behind him.

Her stomach flopped about inside her. What was wrong with her? The smell must remind her of her father, even though he smelled of musk. She shook her head.

Mr. Dawson stood behind his desk, bent over looking at a small makeshift shelf sitting on the floor. "I do not have many, but you are welcome to read any of these." He held out a few books to her.

Zia took the books. She turned them over in her hands, not recognizing either of the titles.

"I have several others, but they are along the same subject lines."

Zia looked up at him. "Who is Alexander Hamilton and this James Monroe? I have never heard of these men."

He stared down at her, one eye slightly more closed the other.

She took an involuntary step back. This man was no different than her father of late. Father had never used intimidation when her mother had been alive. But now he used his strength and his menacing looks to bend her to his will. Fortifying herself against Mr. Dawson's presence, she took back the steps she had given him.

"They are great men. Both were instrumental in the Americans freeing themselves from British rule." He reached for the books. "But if the topic does not interest you..."

Zia pulled the books into her chest. "I did not say I was not interested. I only said I did not know them."

He scowled at her. "They are important to me. If you find you do not care for them, please return them. I should not like to see them misplaced."

Zia was now the one to scowl. "Do you think me irresponsible? I have no intention of losing your books, sir. If there has been something in our brief conversations before now which has led you to these conclusions, I apologize."

His face relaxed. "It is I who should beg your forgiveness. It was rude of me to assume you would be careless."

She gave him one last thoughtful look, then pulled the books away from her chest. "You prefer books on politics then?"

He shrugged. "Not necessarily. We had a fair assortment of books in my family home, growing up. But most of them had to stay behind when I came here with Tad..." He glanced up at her. "Er, Shearsby."

She sat down in the chair across the desk from him, even though he had not asked her to.

His brow creased, but he said nothing.

"You are not from here. That is why you sound different?" Zia set the books in her lap and gave him her full attention.

Mr. Dawson shook his head. "No. I am originally from America. But I came with Shearsby from the West Indies." He reached a hand up and pulled on his earlobe.

"Your heritage is what makes you interested in reading about American politics?" Many different expressions flitted across Mr. Dawson's face and for a moment, Zia thought he might be hiding something.

He shrugged. It seemed to be something he did frequently. "What are your preferences in books?"

"My father prefers I read the scholarly works of Kantemir and others like him." She smiled smugly. "Although, without my father's knowledge, I did read *Voyage to the Isle of Love*. It is the one work by Kantemir's that my father did not wish me to read."

Mr. Dawson quirked a brow. "And he would disapprove of that choice?"

Zia nodded. "Father believes poetry a waste of my time. He says it is fine for other featherbrained girls, but his daughter will have enough knowledge to carry on a conversation and not bore her male suitors." She sighed. "Only his plan did not work. Most gentlemen do not wish to have a wife with a brain in her head. It makes them feel inferior. And men do not like to feel such. Or that is my experience, at least."

Mr. Dawson stared at her and she felt the need to squirm again. "Your father is not here now. What would you choose to read if you had your pick?"

"Oh, a gothic novel." The words were out of her mouth before she had a chance to stop them. What must a man like Mr. Dawson think of such an admission? He already thought her lacking for some reason; what must this new revelation do to her character in his eyes?

His mouth twitched up to one side. "That was not what I expected."

Her face burned even more, but she willed herself not to look away.

"If you are accustomed to reading scholarly works," Mr. Dawson said, "I cannot imagine you would have much trouble comprehending those books." His head inclined toward the books sitting in her lap. "If you have any questions, I would be happy to answer them for you." His face seemed to color up slightly, but that seemed an absurd notion. What did Mr. Dawson have to be embarrassed about?

Zia took this as her cue to leave. She clutched the books to her. "Thank you for allowing me to read these."

"It is my pleasure, *Lady* Zia." Mr. Dawson stood and sketched a shallow bow, but he said nothing more. Why must he make every title sound as if it were bestowed straight from the devil himself?

She turned and hurried from the room, unable to stand the scrutiny she felt in his gaze. Once she cleared the doorway and found the corridor empty, she leaned her back against the wall and took a deep breath. Their conversation, while it had started out terse, had ended on almost friendly terms.

Perhaps Mr. Dawson was not as much like her father as she originally thought. If they could continue to have conversations such as this, perhaps she might even consider him a friend. Dare she even hope, maybe she would not always be so lonely.

CHAPTER 7

Dawson tossed a pile of correspondence on Tad's desk. "I have answered those that required a response, however, the two on top I thought needed your personal attention."

Tad nodded, lifting the letters in question slightly off the desk as he looked them over. He dropped them back down and turned his attention to a paper sitting at his left hand. The paper showed obvious signs of folding. It curled in on itself at several places. He picked it up and stared at it.

A familiar sense of dread squeezed at Dawson's chest. He had seen this exact look on his friend's face many times over the course of their lives. "What? Have you purchased another property on my behalf?" His voice came out wryly, not indicating the panic that started to rise the longer Tad remained silent.

Finally, after what felt like a lifetime, Tad shook his head. "No. It is nothing like that." He tossed the paper across the desk and Dawson grabbed it. What could be in this letter that gave Tad such pause? And then a thought brought a cold sweat to his back and neck. What if something had happened to Tad's mother or sisters back on the farm in Pennsylvania?

Dawson looked to the signature at the bottom of the letter. It did not look familiar. He sank deeper into his chair. "I do not have my glasses with me. Can you just outline the better part of it?" He rubbed at his dry, tired eyes. Being an estate owner had disrupted more than just his sleep.

Tad sat back in his chair and assumed his customary thinking position—fingers steepled and resting at his chin. "I sent a rider with a note to Chatney House."

Dawson's brow crinkled as he tried to place how he knew the name of the estate. His brows slowly rose as he remembered. "You wrote to the Duke of Heathrough and you did not consult me first? She is my guest, Tad. I am responsible for her. How could you take such a high hand?" Where this sudden wave of protectiveness for Lady Zia or rather Miss Petrovich—Dawson still had not decided what to call her—came from, Dawson could not say. In point of fact, it was likely he felt Tad had overstepped. After all, Dawson had his own estate now and Tad did not have the right to interfere with it.

Tad dropped his fingers and leaned his elbows on the desk. "I was only trying to feel the situation out. I was trying to ascertain if he knew about the girl and thought it possible she is telling the truth."

Dawson sighed gruffly. If Tad had not done so much good in Dawson's life, he would be angrier about the *initiative* Tad had taken. But now, he found he just wished to discover the contents of the letter.

"What did he say?"

Tad motioned to the paper with his head. "He says he does have a niece by the name of Zia, but that it is doubtful she is come to England. He believes the girl's father would have sent word of her travels to him."

"Not if the girl ran away, as she claims. I am guessing her father does not have a notion where she is currently, and so could not send word." A niggle of doubt about Zia and her bouncers wormed away inside his stomach. Could she be telling the truth? "Did he give a description of his niece? Give any indication of how we might discover if this girl is, indeed, who she claims to be?"

Tad shook his head. "No. As I suspected, he has never laid eyes upon her before. His sister never returned to England once she married the Russian prince."

Dawson sunk down in his chair. "It is possible one of the two women traveling in the coach could very possibly be a princess. But how do we know that it is not the woman buried in the churchyard?"

Tad shook his head. "I do not know. I had my father's signet ring to give credence to my claims, but..." He did not finish the sentence.

"And you look almost identical to your father. It is not hard to see the similarities." Dawson ran a hand over the back of his neck. "Perhaps that same notion will hold true for the duke's sister and her daughter? But how would we find a picture of the woman?"

"Surely there is one at Chatney House," Tad said.

Dawson sighed. "We are left with more questions than before you inserted yourself into this matter."

"So it would seem," Tad muttered.

Dawson could not think on the matter any longer. He had an estate to run, and a mother to tend to. "I am to go into the village today. My mother would like to visit a few shops; I think she is also wanting to discover what types of associations might be available to her. I had not considered what she was to lose by joining me over here. She has lost all her friends." He scrubbed a hand over his face. "As you are fully aware, I am not much of a conversationalist and my company lacks greatly."

"Of that I am painfully aware." Tad grinned. "I am sure there are a great many people who are anxious to make your mother's acquaintance. They just do not know it yet."

Dawson let out a sigh. "I hope I did the right thing in bringing her here."

Violet knocked on the door and pushed it open slightly. "Good morning, Dawson. How are you today?"

Dawson stood and bowed to her. "Very well, Your Grace. And you?"

She waved him away. "I find I am quite well. The sun isn't quite shining, but the temperature is warmer than it was yesterday. I plan to take a turn about the maze this afternoon."

Dawson smiled. The duchess always seemed to find something to be happy about. Even on a cold, drizzly November day.

"How is your guest doing? Tad says she has awakened. I should love to have the three of you over for supper."

Dawson nodded. "We should be honored to come."

Violet nodded. "Tomorrow evening? I shall have some card tables set up as well."

"Will there be need for more than one table?" Tad asked. "By my count, there will only be five us and I am more than content to sit out a hand or two."

Violet's brow wrinkled and her lips pursed into a line. "Have you forgotten already, Tad?"

Tad's eyes widened slightly, and Dawson could see his brain working. Violet let out an exasperated sigh. "Rose and Oliver arrive tomorrow. They will be staying on with us through the holidays, until we all travel to London."

"Is it time for their visit already?"

Violet scowled—or came as close to scowling as Violet ever

seemed to manage—at her husband. "You get on well with Oliver, and even Rose, most of the time. Do not pretend you are dreading the visit."

Tad went to his wife and put his hands on her shoulders, running them down the lengths of her arms. "I am doing no such thing. I had only lost track of the days. I will be most happy to see your sister and Lord Munsford again. It should make traveling to London much more enjoyable."

She softened toward him. "Then I shall see that the card tables are put up for tomorrow evening." She glanced over at Dawson as she turned to leave. "Give your mother my regards, Dawson. Oh, and..." Her gaze flicked to Tad.

He shrugged.

"And to your guest."

Dawson nodded. "I shall." Before she could reach the doorway, Dawson called after her. "Your Grace?"

She stopped. "Yes?"

"We are to make a trip into the village today. If you are in need of anything, just send word and I would be happy to fetch it for you."

"I shall keep that in mind. Thank you, Dawson."

Silence filled the room when the door closed behind her.

"Lady Zia likes to read." Dawson sat for a moment, letting those words sink in.

"How very unique of her." Tad grinned and sat down behind his desk.

"My point being, I have no library, and thus, very few books to offer her." He put his elbows on the arms of the chair and leaned his body slightly forward. "Perhaps she could borrow something from your library when we visit tomorrow?"

Tad nodded. "I do not see a problem. We only suspect her of telling falsehoods, not being a thief."

Dawson bristled at Tad's assertion, but he did not know why exactly. Did not Dawson think she was lying to him? Why should he feel offended when Tad voiced Dawson's own beliefs?

He pushed himself to standing and moved toward the door, a sudden desire to go gripping hold of him. "I should be on my way. I do not wish to have my mother waiting on me." He did not even allow Tad a word before he was out the door and making his way toward the stables.

Dawson entered Fawnbrooke; the sound of his mother humming drifted down the staircase. He paused in his tracks as he was immediately struck by the feeling of home. Not since leaving his family home the night he learned his father had lost the house in a single hand of cards had he felt this way. Not even Tad's family home had felt this way.

But here he was, standing in the entryway of his home. His chest expanded and his whole body relaxed. What made a place feel like this? Could it be because this home was his? Or perhaps it was because of his mother's presence? Likely it was a combination of both. He shook his head. He would never have guessed that England could ever feel like home.

The humming grew louder as his mother came ever closer to the upstairs landing. He smiled until he saw Miss Petrovich descend the stairs. How had he thought the voice belonged to his mother?

Dawson headed straight for his study and lowered himself into a rickety chair by the fireplace, careful not to make any jarring movements and risk the chair coming apart at the joints. He let his mind think on Miss Petrovich. Was it not the humming that made him think of home? He rubbed his palm back and forth over the arm of the chair. What was he so worried about? It was not as if the woman's humming meant anything. She was practically a stranger. It had merely jogged a memory. That is all.

He absently rubbed at his chest. Yes, it was just the memory he treasured.

His mind turned to his conversation with Tad. Why did the letter from the Duke of Heathrough make Dawson's stomach sink? Had he secretly hoped to have his belief discounted? And why had he felt the need to defend Miss Petrovich to Tad? That he was so concerned over the matter, concerned him the most. The more he thought on it, the more it consumed him, and his earlier ease drifted away.

Dawson pushed himself up with a grunt, then cringed as the chair wobbled and creaked. He moved the rest of the way to his feet with much slower and gentler movements.

He needed air to clear his thoughts. Perhaps now would be a good time to take his mother into the village. Surely that would help take his mind off those things he had no business thinking about.

Dawson went directly into the North Parlor, knowing his mother would be inside. He did not, however, count on Miss Petrovich being there as well. She was curled up with a rug over her lap, in his mother's favorite window seat, her nose in a book.

His mother sat on the sofa, her stitchery in hand. Dawson looked between the two women, sitting almost as far apart as two people could get in the room. What did it mean? Did they not get on well? And why did that notion bother him?

He bypassed Miss Petrovich and sat next to his mother. She laid her stitchery to the side and turned slightly toward him. She reached up a hand and placed it on his cheek. "Why do I never see you smile anymore? Is that not why you shaved off the beard?"

Dawson smirked. "Because we have lived an ocean away for more than two years."

She tsked. "You know what I am alluding to, Son."

He shrugged. "I smile, Mother. There is just much to do and not enough time nor money to do it. I feel the weight of it continually."

She put her fabric into the basket on the floor. "How can I help? I am not so old as to be unable to assist you in some things. Put me to work." She glanced at her sampler lying in the basket. "All this sitting about doing nothing is quite tiresome."

Dawson smiled genuinely. "I have missed you, Mother. But I am afraid you will need to get used to more sitting about than you are used to. I am a gentleman now. And no gentleman's mother would be working as you have these last years."

She huffed out a sigh and settled into the seat back. "Could I at least purchase some fabric and work at stitching me a dress or two?"

Dawson frowned. Even that would not be looked upon with favor among much of England's upper class.

"What if I promise to hide it away, should any visitors stop by?"

Dawson relaxed and let his shoulders drop a fraction. Had he really become so concerned about what those in society thought of him? And if so, when had this change occurred? He would need to see to it that he changed back to his demeanor of disdain for all things *society* related.

"I believe I can scrape up enough money to buy you some fabric. We will see what we can find when we go to the village. Perhaps when Tad and I go to Tattersalls come the first of the year, I can purchase you some finer fabric than is to be found here in Leicestershire."

His mother's smile and the light in her eyes was all he needed to know that this was a good plan.

His mother patted him on the cheek and then stood up. "I am to check on Alice in the kitchen. I think in a short time she will make a very proficient cook, but the girl still lacks confidence."

She left Dawson sitting on the sofa by himself. He looked over his shoulder at Miss Petrovich. Her legs were drawn up, a rug draped over them and the cushion she sat on. The book, while he could not see it now, must still have been open on her legs, but she was not looking at it. Her focus was on him; she did not even pretend to look away when he glanced back and caught her staring. Would everything she did surprise him?

He turned back, unable to maintain eye contact with her for long. Besides, his neck was starting to ache from the position. He should inform his new housekeeper—it still seemed so odd to think he had a housekeeper—to ready his carriage, or rather, Tad's carriage. It was on loan to Dawson until he could afford one of his own.

Movement at the settee across from him drew his attention. Miss Petrovich had removed herself from the window seat and now took up residence across from him. Had she come over to talk with him or simply because his mother had quit the room?

She bit her lower lip, clenching it between her teeth. "You said I could ask you questions about these books?"

Dawson nodded. "If I know the answer, I will gladly share it with you."

She nodded. "These men, they are politicians?"

Dawson nodded again.

"Mr. Hamilton was in favor of the—" She looked down and thumbed through a few pages of the book. "Continental Congress."

Dawson nodded. "Yes. He became a strong advocate for the

new federal government after the war ended and the constitution was adopted."

Her brow furrowed. "It seems to me he was taking a great risk by expressing such views."

"Yes, he was. There were many still loyal to the crown." Dawson sighed. "I am sorry I do not have more interesting books for you."

She shook her head. "These are agreeable. I thank you very much for allowing me to read them."

He stared at her. This uncertain, almost shy woman seemed more in line with her station. Perhaps, when her guard was down, she forgot to act like the spoiled princess she had claimed to be earlier. "Perhaps when we next go to Morley Park, you may borrow something from the duke's library that is more to your liking."

She smiled. "If not, I shall be content with these."

"My mother and I will be traveling into the village after tea. If you have your letter ready, I shall be happy to post it for you."

Her bottom lip was captured in her teeth again. "Would it be possible for me to make the trip also? I should like to post the letter myself and perhaps check the local dress shop." She held up the skirt of her gown. "I shall need more than one dress to wear...until my uncle comes for me."

Why the pause after the word wear? Was she not confident her *uncle* would come for her once he received her letter? Or, perhaps she knew he would not come because he was not her uncle. Could her letter simply be telling the duke of the death of his niece in the accident?

It seemed to be a pattern as of late; Dawson had more questions than he did answers.

CHAPTER 8

Zia pulled the tassel hanging from the end of her reticule through her lightly clenched hand and then wrapped it around her index finger. It fell away and she began again. If her mother could see her now, she'd surely be frowning over the poor way she was handling herself. *A princess does not fidget.* How many times had she heard those words throughout her childhood? And yet, she did not seem able to stop herself. She had fidgeted more in the last few days than in the entirety of her life.

While she had not begun her associations with Mr. Dawson and his mother on a lie, she was, even now, becoming the very thing they believed her to be. She did have a letter to post, but it was not to her uncle.

Every time she sat at the small table in her chambers to put words to paper, she had not been able to do it. Writing the letter to Tiana's mother had taken everything Zia had. There had been nothing left for her uncle. Especially when she was at such a loss as to what she might say to him. Zia had been uncertain of her uncle's reception of her before; the Duke of Shearsby's comments had only increased her doubts.

Zia amended her thoughts. While the *words* the duke had used were not overly concerning, it was the tone in which he had delivered them that left her feeling so unmoored. So much doubt had come through in those few words—a doubt which now seemed to cripple Zia's ability to move forward with her original plan. All she seemed to manage was living day to day, accepting what each presented.

Zia looked out the window, not seeing any of the scenery passing before her. Her fingers tangled in the fringe and Zia looked down to discover she had worried the tassel into a large knot. She grumbled low in her throat and began working to untangle the fringe.

While she did not know what her father would do when he found her, she knew what Prince Sokolov was capable of doing. She rubbed lightly over her cheek with a gloved hand. She had felt his displeasure before. And that was only for speaking when he had not asked for her to do so. Sokolov did not share her father's opinion on well-educated women. Or perhaps he just objected to the notion of a woman *sharing* her knowledge. She was most certain he would have no tolerance for a woman crying off an attachment and making him look the fool. Zia shuttered when she thought what he would do to her.

"Are you cold, my lady?" Mrs. Dawson looked mildly concerned.

"I am well, thank you." Her words were more clipped than she had intended, as she had been drawn from her thoughts unexpectedly.

"Why did you not wear the heavier cloak? Is it not in your wardrobe?" Mr. Dawson looked at her. Was that concern or skepticism in his look?

Zia took in a jerky breath. "Tiana was wearing that cloak when she—" Zia could not say the word. She knew she should have accepted Tiana's fate and moved beyond it by now, but she found the task more difficult than she had anticipated. "I am not sure I shall ever be able to wear my cloak again. No matter how cold I am."

Mr. Dawson squinted at her, as if he could ferret out a lie from her words. If she kept fiddling with the tassel, he would be even more convinced of her deception. She dropped it and clasped her hands together. "Thank you for bringing me along. I believe the fresh air will do me good."

Both mother and son only dipped their heads in acknowledgement.

The carriage came to a stop and Zia could hardly stay seated until the footman wrenched open the door. The cold bit at her nose as she was handed down from the carriage, working its way through her gown and underclothes. Gooseflesh flared leaving no smooth skin on her body.

She pulled the useless cloak tighter about her, feeling greater sorrow that Tiana had worn this cloak for so long without saying a word. How had Zia not noticed? She put her head down and moved down the walk.

"The posting house is that direction." Mr. Dawson's voice stopped her in her tracks. She looked up to see him pointing in the opposite direction.

She turned and nodded. "Thank you." She trudged a few rods down the walk and pushed into the inn Mr. Dawson had indicated.

The warmth from the fire roaring at the far end of the common area brought a tingle to her cheeks. She worked her mouth several times, trying to force the blood to circulate and warm them up.

A woman in an apron scurried up to her. "May I help ye, miss?"

Zia stood completely still for a moment before she reached into her reticule and withdrew the letter. "I have a letter to post."

She nodded over to a long counter area where an older man pushed through a curtain and disappeared behind it. "Me husband would be the one to handle your post."

Zia offered a small smile, remembering the way Tiana had interacted with the serving class. Perhaps she would do well to use similar tactics today. "Thank you." She walked over to the counter and waited for the innkeeper.

He returned a moment later and stood behind the counter in front of her. Zia thrust the letter forward. "I need to post this."

He looked at her scrawl on the front and whistled. "Russia, eh, miss?" He turned the letter over and then back. "Never seen no other letters addressed to Russia."

"You are able to send it, though, are you not?"

He nodded and told her the fee.

She opened her reticule and placed the coins on the counter. He dropped the coins into a box and put the letter in a pile. He turned to return to the back room, but Zia stopped him.

"Begging your pardon."

He turned back with raised brows but did not return to the counter.

Zia fumbled with her reticule. "I was curious if I were to post a letter to Derbyshire, how long until it would be received?" The information would give her an idea of how long she was safe...or at least relatively safe.

"Depending on the weather, miss, not more than a couple of days. Do ye have another letter to post?"

Zia shook her head. "My letter is not yet ready. I was only curious." She dipped her head and turned to leave. She regretted leaving the warmth of the inn as soon as the door opened.

Glancing down the street, she looked for the dress shop or the Dawsons. Both options made her equally anxious and excited.

Her eyes found the sign for the shop, swinging in the breeze. It was on the same side of the street and only a few shops down. Zia hurried, hoping to get into the shop before all of the heat from the inn left her.

She pushed through the door, leaning her back against it once it was shut again. This shop was not as warm as the inn, but it was still a welcome relief.

She took in a deep breath and moved about the shop. There were bolts of fabric, which should make Mrs. Dawson happy. Zia felt a grudging admiration toward the lady for knowing how to make a gown. Zia had not the first notion how to do such a thing. She clutched at her reticule, feeling the paper money she had stitched inside the lining for safety. It would not buy a new wardrobe, but it should get her two or three day dresses. She did not believe she would need a ball gown, at least not while staying with the Dawsons. She had explored small sections of Fawn-brooke, and it seemed the ballroom lacked a roof.

If she ended up at her uncle's estate, a ball gown may be necessary then. But that was a worry for another day.

She walked around the store looking at the gowns on display. They were nothing to the gowns that had been destroyed in the accident, but at least they would provide some variety to her wardrobe.

Zia selected a dress in a lovely shade of blue and one in green, the same shade as the emerald pendant her mother had given to her. She swallowed hard, regretting leaving it behind in Odessa. At the time she had not thought it important, but now it felt as if she had left her mother behind too. Curious how her thoughts had changed.

She gathered both dresses and moved to the shopkeeper at the back. She placed the gowns on the counter. "I should like to purchase these."

The woman looked her up and down. "I do not issue credit."

Zia scowled at the woman. How dare she think Zia a common woman with no means. If there were any other option, Zia would leave now and give her business to someone else. But this was the only dress shop in the village, as far as Zia had seen. "I shall not be needing credit, madam." Zia carefully pulled the thread holding the lining shut, causing the inside of the reticule to bunch up. Zia used her teeth to cut the thread and the lining fell open. She retrieved the stack of bank notes and took several off the top. "I shall be purchasing these and—" She turned and moved to a table with bolts of fabric. Picking a pale pink one, with tiny white flowers, she placed it on the counter as well. "And this also, please."

The woman eyed the bank notes and nodded, her tone now accommodating and kind. "Shall I schedule you for a fitting? I am sure these will need alterations."

Zia fixed the woman with the most princess gaze she had, one that her mother had taught her. The one that never failed to put people in their proper place. "No. I have someone very capable of making the alterations for me. I shall not be in need of your assistance." Zia swallowed the fear that Mrs. Dawson would decline and leave Zia with ill-fitting gowns. She also hoped the older woman was as skilled a seamstress as she had alluded. They did not seem to get on so well. But with the way the shopkeeper had treated her, Zia would wear a sack before asking the woman for help.

The woman wrapped and bundled Zia's things, her brows knitted together. Several times she glanced up at Zia, but then shook her head and returned to her work. She handed the package over and Zia exchanged it for a banknote.

A hand reached forward and grabbed the parcel from her hands. Zia jerked around, a shout forming on her lips. Mr. Dawson smiled tightly at her and then at the lady behind the counter.

"May I carry this for you, *Princess?*" His voice held a note of mocking, but from the way the woman behind the counter raised her brows, Zia thought she might have been the only one to notice. Her cheeks burned. How long had he been behind her? How much of the conversation had he heard? He had not been there when she returned to the tables for the bolt of fabric. Or had he? She could not be sure as she had not been looking for him.

He dipped his head and placed his hand at the small of her back, giving her a gentle nudge toward the door. The warmth from his hand spread up her back and she barely noticed the cold as they stepped outside. Was it normal for a tingling sensation to accompany warmth? She had never noticed such a thing until now. Perhaps it was due to the extreme cold followed by the excessive warmth of the shop, only to return to the excessive cold again. Such drastic changes in temperature must surely be the reason she felt so jittery.

"It is not wise to display blunt so openly. If you are not careful, you will bring every highwayman out of retirement and cause more to take up the occupation."

"Highwaymen?" Her voice came out oddly breathy. "I knew it. It was just as I told Tiana." She clutched her reticule closer to her body. "Why do you think it was sewn into the lining, sir, if not to keep it hidden?"

He looked heavenward. "There are too many flaws in your thinking for me to even begin to tell you of them."

She let out a little huff. Who did he think he was, speaking to her in this way? But then, this was how he always seemed to speak with her. A vexing notion, at best. "Please? I do not wish to tax you excessively, but perhaps you could tell me of just one error in my thinking?"

He let out a grunt-laugh. "For one, if a person is to rob you, he will not ask you to withdraw the money from your reticule. He will simply take the whole bag. Thus, having it sewn into the lining of the bag is not the best of plans." He cleared his throat and glanced down at her. "Not to mention the bulk that the money adds to the reticule. It is as if you are telling the world, 'I have blunt stashed inside. Please, come relieve me of it, good sir.'"

Her mouth dropped open, but she found herself unable to speak. He had made some valid points, but must he reveal them to her as if she were a dolt? Her face burned. How had she not seen the silliness in her plan? Would it not have been wiser to sew the money into the lining of her cloak or somewhere less obvious?

Perhaps he was correct to speak to her as if she were a small child of little wit. She dropped her head and walked quickly beside him, nearly having to run to match his long stride. Looking back on all that had happened, it seemed that a child *had* hatched her plan of escape. And now poor Tiana was buried in the churchyard.

"Did you get what you needed, *Princess*?" He did not look at her, but kept his gaze trained straight ahead.

She stopped and stomped her foot. A small grain of satisfaction planted in her chest when he was forced to stop also. "You need not use my title, sir." She forced the words through clenched teeth, even as she looked around to see who might be listening. The dark clouds forming in the sky seemed to have driven most people to their homes. "Especially when we are in public. I had rather hoped to keep it a secret whilst in England. Or at least until I arrived at my uncle's estate. It will certainly come out then, as I am sure he will throw a ball or some such extravagance, in my honor."

"There can be no doubt he will." Mr. Dawson nodded and continued walking, quickly leaving her behind.

Zia picked up her skirts and hurried to catch up.

"Very well," he said. "What shall I call you then? Was it not you who told me your title in the first place?"

"I already told you to call me Lady Zia." She sighed heavily, unhappy that it sounded more like a pout. *Princesses do not pout. They command. Pouting only makes one seem weak.* Her father had ingrained that in her since she was a child. But it did not seem to matter in this situation. Mr. Dawson did not appear to be paying her any mind. How could he when he was at least a rod ahead of her?

They arrived at the carriage and he handed her parcel off to the driver who promptly stowed it away before opening the coach door. Mr. Dawson offered his hand and helped Zia into the carriage before lifting himself in.

Zia noted that Mrs. Dawson was already seated with a rug tucked about her legs. She smiled tightly at Zia.

Zia frowned. Like mother like son, apparently.

"I find I prefer princess to Lady Zia," Mr. Dawson said, "but I shall abide your wishes." He settled onto the bench next to his mother, but his gaze never left Zia's face. "You never answered my earlier question as to whether you had purchased all you needed. But it is no matter now. We are leaving before the weather turns. If you did not get all you came for, we shall try to make another trip once this storm blows through." Mr. Dawson rapped on the side of the carriage and moments later it lurched forward.

"Were you able to post the letter to your uncle?" The hope in Mrs. Dawson's voice was unmistakable.

Zia bit her bottom lip and nodded. "Yes. I did post my letter.

Although, I am sure this storm will slow the delivery down." Zia turned her head toward the window. Why had she not told them the truth? They already thought her a cracker, and now she had proven them correct.

She dropped her head against the window. Tiana would know how to proceed. Why did Tiana have to leave her?

CHAPTER 9

Dawson slapped the paper-wrapped package on the palm of his hand. What had he been thinking? The decision to buy two gothic novels while in town yesterday had been rash and ill-thought out.

He had told himself that his mother would enjoy the books, but he had never seen his mother read such books in the entirety of his life. Miss Petrovich was the only person he knew who desired a gothic novel. He furrowed his brow. It was possible Tad's cousin, Miss Standish, might like such books, but the notion she would come to Fawnbrooke in search of such a book was preposterous.

He should just seek out Miss Petrovich and give them to her. Be done with the whole situation.

He put his hand on the arms of his chair to lift himself up, but halfway to standing, he dropped back into his chair. What was he to say to her? Any of the words he had rehearsed in his mind seemed ridiculous. He was not some love-struck boy mooning over a girl. And yet, every time he thought about giving her the books, his stomach did a jig, the likes of which he had never before experienced.

Dawson slammed the package down on his desk. "Damnation."

A chuckle sounded from the doorway. "What has you in such a dither? I have not seen you scowl this fiercely since our arrival in this *dratted* country."

Dawson smirked at Tad. "Are you just to stand about looking like an idiot, or are you to come and sit down?"

Tad moved into the study, his grin covering his entire face.

It only served to make Dawson glower more. How was he to explain his mood to his friend? Should he tell him of his ill-conceived purchases? He was sure the duke would laugh him out of the county.

Tad sat in the seat opposite Dawson and slouched down into it. Dawson raised a brow.

Tad shrugged. "It is the only way I can make this chair in any way comfortable."

The duke's discomfort did tug a small smile to Dawson's lips. "I assume you came here for a reason, Tad."

He nodded but waved his hand, as if to push his reason away. "We can get to that later. Now, I wish to know what has you spouting curses that would surely earn you a lecture, should Mother D hear them."

Dawson grunted. Why did Tad feel it his right to wheedle every last secret and detail from Dawson? "It is a private matter. I assure you; I can handle it on my own."

Tad narrowed his gaze. "From the look on your face, I should disagree with that assessment. And I believe I know at least the root of the problem."

Dawson snorted and leaned his elbows on his desk, propping his chin in his hands. "Please, enlighten me."

Tad nodded. "I think it has to do with your Russian princess."

Dawson clenched his jaw tight, his lips pressed into a tight line. How could he know? Dawson had told no one about purchasing the books for Miss Petrovich. "Please, do continue, Your Grace."

Tad laughed. "When you start *your gracing* me, I know I am on the right track." He stared at Dawson, as if he could discover the truth simply by watching him.

Dawson dropped his hands to the desk, the brown package brushing against them. He picked up the package and moved it to the side, placing a stack of papers on top of it, before returning his gaze to his friend.

Tad grinned, his head nodding. "You visited the bookshop while you were in the village."

It wasn't a question, so Dawson felt no inclination to respond. Besides, the more he spoke on this subject, the greater the chance that Tad would actually figure out the source of his discomfort.

"I am going to take your silence as a yes."

Dawson growled. Why could he not leave it alone?

"There does not happen to be gothic novels in that brown paper wrapper, does there, Dawson?"

"And what if there are?" Dawson snapped. "I think it the only way I will get my books back, by giving her something more to her liking. Besides, I thought my mother might enjoy them. I also bought one by 'A Lady.' I believe you bought the same book for your cousin, Miss Standish." He looked pointedly at Tad. "Is not a well-rounded library what all gentlemen aspire to? Besides, it would be silly of me to buy books just for Miss Petrovich. It is not as if she will be staying for much longer. She posted a letter to her uncle just yesterday."

Tad nodded, but the twitching of his lips made Dawson want to throw something at him.

"I am pleased to see you are taking your efforts to become a gentleman seriously at last." He cast a look at the package buried under the stack of papers. "You will have to inform me of how the lady likes your well-rounded library."

Dawson glared at Tad. "Why was it you came again, Your Grace? Is your love life so bad that you must meddle in mine?"

The duke's eyes dropped to his hands, no trace of humor left on his face.

Dawson sat forward. "What is it? Is there something wrong with you and Violet?"

A heavy sigh sounded from Tad's lips. "It has been two years and still there are no children in our immediate future. Each pregnancy that is lost..." He cleared his throat. "It has been hard on Violet. I am afraid she believes it her fault."

"I am sorry, Tad. I had no idea." Dawson ran a hand through his hair. He preferred it when Tad was laughing at him as opposed to this. "Is there anything to be done?"

"The doctors advise her to rest and not overexert herself. But I think it just words."

Tad shifted in his seat. "Now, what were we discussing? Ah, yes. Your lovely Russian princess."

The mood in the room shifted and Dawson was happy to feel it.

Tad pushed himself upright and wiggled around, as if trying to find the right spot. "Violet wished me to remind you about dinner tonight. Although, it will likely not be cards. The weather has delayed Munsford and Rose. It shall only be the five of us."

Dawson nodded. "I do not mind, but if Her Grace should like to wait until her sister arrives, I am amiable to that as well."

Tad's brow rose. "I should never have thought you to welcome Rose's company."

Dawson shrugged. "Since her marriage, she has become more tolerable, from what little I have seen of her."

Tad nodded. "It is true, though I should never have guessed it to be so." Tad let out a breath. "Violet claims Rose is back to being the sister she remembers from their youth." He shrugged. "I am still doubtful of her complete transformation, but I shall endeavor to give her the benefit of the doubt."

Dawson drummed his fingers on the desk. "Is that all? You look as though there is more on your mind."

Tad waved his concern away. "We need to discuss our trip to Somerton's estate, but it can wait." He looked at Dawson. "Have you changed your mind about joining us in London after Twelfth Night? I am sure your mother would enjoy the London Season."

Dawson nodded. "I am sure she would find it diverting enough. But there is too much to do here this year. Perhaps when the estate is turning a profit, London might be considered. But not now. I shall only have time to make the visit to Tattersalls and then will return immediately."

"I knew it to be like this, but I had hoped it could be different." Tad sighed. "Who am I to have intelligent conversation with if you are not there?"

Dawson grinned. "I have heard tell that the duchess is a remarkable conversationalist."

Tad's face relaxed into an almost lovesick smile. "Yes, you are correct. I should like to spend all my time speaking with her. But alas, they will not allow her into Brooks's."

Dawson clenched his fist. "If you will recall, they would not allow *me* into Brooks's either. It seems you will have to be content with Munsford's company. And did you not say the Duke of Heathrough proved diverting at times?"

Tad sighed again. "But it is not the same. I will miss you this season, my friend."

Dawson felt a small tug in his chest and grunted. "It is not as if we are courting, Tad. You will return to Morley Park in July and all will be as it should. Perhaps, you will even be able to see a few changes here at Fawnbrooke."

Tad grinned. "'It is not as if we are courting.' You are always one to speak it as it is, Dawson. Indeed, I shall hardly miss seeing your disobliging countenance." He pushed himself up and moved toward the door. "I shall have to endure it several months more, I suppose. I do not know how I shall tolerate it."

Dawson stared at Tad's retreating frame. "It is I who shall be counting down the days, Your Grace."

Tad stopped at the doorway. "Until supper then." He bowed deep and walked out of the room.

Dawson sat at his desk shaking his head. "The man is daft." But even as he said it, he knew he didn't mean it. Tad was the best man he had ever known.

The brown wrapping peeked out from under the papers on his desk. Dawson sighed as he moved them aside. "May as well get this over with." He had made some valid arguments with Tad—ones he had not previously thought on. Surely he could make Miss Petrovich see that these books were not a sign of any partiality on his part. But if he was so convinced it did not show his preference toward her, why did he feel the need to keep insisting as much? Who was he trying to convince if not himself?

He shook his head with a grunt and stood up, his chair scraping loudly on the floor. Where to find Miss Petrovich? Would she be in the North Parlor with his mother again or had the two of them decided to keep to different rooms?

It was a shame really, that the two of them did not get on better. Dawson knew, even though his mother had never mentioned it, that she had wished to have a daughter. She had looked on Tad's sisters as quite her own. He knew it must be difficult for her now, with both Ainsley and Sarah back in Pennsylvania.

He had thought Miss Petrovich may help fill that void. But he appeared to be wrong on that notion.

Walking to the parlor, he found his mother by the fire, her stitching in her lap.

Dawson scanned the rest of the room, relieved when he saw Miss Petrovich sitting in the window seat. Again, she had a rug tucked about her with her legs drawn up. It seemed she had taken a liking to the window seat as well. And they were both in the same room together. Did that not mean there was hope? Could two people who disliked each other really stay in the same room together for hours on end?

Dawson chose to think it a starting point to them forming a bond of friendship. Time would only tell if his thinking was correct. But then, why did he care? Was not Miss Petrovich's time with them drawing to an end? Surely, Heathrough would be coming for her before week's end. Unless, of course, Heathrough did not actually know this woman.

Then what would Dawson do with her?

CHAPTER 10

Zia sat in her normal spot in the parlor, her legs bent up in front of her and a rug tucked about her. Her book sat propped up on her legs, but she had yet to read a single word.

Her eyes flicked often to the back of Mrs. Dawson's head as she sat sewing on the sofa. *Why am I so afraid to speak with her? I am a princess, am I not? It is she who should cower at the thought of speaking to me.*

And yet, Zia could not bring herself to move from her spot in the window.

It had been a full day since they went to the village, and Zia had yet to approach Mrs. Dawson about helping her alter the gowns she had purchased. She looked at the dress she had worn since her arrival here at Fawnbrooke. The maid, Lucy, had done a fair job at keeping it clean and fresh, but Zia was sick to death of staring at what she had once found delightfully charming little daisies. Now the small flowers seemed to mock her.

The door of the sitting room pushed open with a low groan. Was there no place on this estate not in need of repair?

Mr. Dawson stepped inside, his eyes darting about the room until they landed on her.

Her heart and her stomach wrestled about inside her, neither seeming to know where they wished to rest permanently. Zia's brow puckered.

Mr. Dawson moved to his mother and placed a quick kiss on her cheek, mumbling something quietly to her before he rose and moved in Zia's direction.

Zia dropped her eyes to her book, pretending to pay him no mind, yet the shallowness of her breathing belied the notion. What was he to speak with her about? Would he ask her about her uncle? She tempered her breathing. Surely, he knew it was too soon yet for a reply.

He stopped in front of her with his hand clasped behind his back.

Zia glanced up at him from beneath her lashes.

He rocked several times on his heels, his face creased in thought.

Why was he not speaking? The longer he stood there, staring at her, the faster her heart raced. His expression did not look as though this was to be an amiable conversation. Not that they'd had many such conversations.

His mouth was turned downward, set in a hard frown. His jaw worked furiously. Finally, he opened his mouth and Zia's pulse ticked up even more.

"I found these while in the village yesterday." He brought his hands forward, a bundle wrapped in brown paper clutched tightly. "That is to say, they are not yours," he quickly added, his eyes looking at everything around her, but never settling on her. "I bought them for my library. After our discussion the other day, I realized how woefully lacking my library is." He grimaced. "Not that one could call what I have a library, by any notion. But I plan to increase it, gradually." He practically threw the package at her. "Anyhow, I thought you might like to be the first to read them."

When she had a secure hold on the books, he dipped his head and turned away, his stride much faster than when he had arrived. She was barely able to say *thank you* before he was out the door.

Zia dropped the book off her lap and onto the bench. Dropping her legs, she pushed her feet out from under the rug. She swiveled and let them hang down from the window seat. If she were only a hand or two taller, her feet might actually touch the floor. But they did not; instead they dangled just above it. She turned the package over in her hands, tugging at the twine holding the paper closed. When the last loop was free, the paper fell away, revealing a deep blue, leather cover, the words pressed with gold lettering. Zia ran her fingers over the title of the top book. *A Sicilian Romance.*

She smiled. A gothic novel, just as she had told him she wished to read. She set aside the two volumes, turning the other books over in her hands so she could see their spines. The *Mysteries of Udolpho*, in four volumes, and *Emma* stared up at her. It seemed all the books Mr. Dawson had purchased in the village were for her. She corrected herself. They were not *for* her, but perhaps she had been on his mind when he purchased them? The notion warmed her completely and she again rubbed her fingers over the titles. Had anyone ever done such a thing for her?

Her mother and father had bought her books and other kinds of trinkets, usually at great cost. But had they ever bought her something she truly wanted and desired? She shook her head. She must stop thinking as though these books were a gift for her. Mr. Dawson had made it very clear he had only been purchasing titles for his fledgling library. She must not make more of this than it was.

She folded the paper neatly into a small square and wound the twine around it. Tucking it in between two of the books, she set the stack aside and took up the top book. She opened the cover, loving the smell of leather, paper, glue and ink as they all mingled together. The book gave a small crack as the spine opened all the way for the first time.

She read the title page of *The Mysteries of Udolpho,* settled back into the corner of the bench, and pulled her legs up to her once again. With one hand, she tucked the rug about her, while the other hand held the book open, her eyes never leaving the page.

She had only completed the first page when she heard the door open again. Surely it was only Mrs. Dawson going to ring for tea or fetch some more thread for her sewing. Zia ignored the sounds, already relishing the book.

A throat cleared and she grudgingly raised her eyes. Mr. Dawson stood in the room again. She glanced down at the book and grinned. She must be enjoying it very much for her not to *feel* Mr. Dawson's presence in the room, as she did on every other occasion.

His mother looked up at him expectantly.

"I forgot to mention it earlier, but we have been invited to dine at Morley Park tonight. The carriage shall be ready to depart at seven. Please meet in the entryway." He smiled at his mother, but only managed to give Zia a slight nod before he turned to quit the room again.

Yes, she had made too much out of the books. Would someone with even the slightest partiality look on her with such disdain? Perhaps disdain was too strong a word. But there was nothing in his behavior, outside of him giving her the books, to indicate he thought of her often.

"The invitation has been extended to include you, as well, Princ...Lady Zia." Mr. Dawson stood by the door, looking at her expectantly.

Dinner with the duke and duchess? Zia looked down at her dress. While Mrs. Dawson had done a fine job mending it, it was a walking dress, not something one would wear to supper with a duke. Zia swallowed. She could not wait any longer to ask for help with the alterations. She needed to wear one of the new gowns this evening. In reality, it was questionable if the alterations could even be finished before tonight. Why had she hesitated so long in asking?

"Thank you. I should be honored to attend with you and your mother."

Mr. Dawson nodded and turned and left the room.

There was no more time for cowering in the window seat, as much as Zia wished to remain there reading. She needed to ask Mrs. Dawson for help. If the woman would not help her, then perhaps Lucy could be of assistance. Although, Zia had no notion if the girl was handy with a needle or not.

Zia stacked the books together grudgingly, noticing the books Mr. Dawson had first loaned her. She would need to deliver them back to his study later.

She pushed herself to leave the safety of the window seat. Clasping her hands in front of her, she walked toward the sofa where Mrs. Dawson sat. Once she arrived in front of the woman, Zia found herself at a loss for words. This had never happened to her before. She licked her lips. *I am a princess. I am not cowed by anyone.*

Mrs. Dawson paused in her sewing, the needle and fabric laying still in her lap. "Yes?"

Zia moistened her lips again. "What are you making?"

She looked up. "Mrs. Bryse told me of a young woman close to delivering a babe. She is in need of many necessities before the babe arrives. I thought to make this gown for it."

"But you do not know the woman?" Zia had not known anyone to do such a thing for a perfect stranger.

"I will meet her when I deliver the gown. What better way to introduce myself to her?"

"Would it be possible for me to accompany you?" Zia did not know why she asked to go along, other than she wished to see the reactions of those on both sides of the gift giving.

Zia twisted her hands together. She needed to stop delaying any long. "I need assistance. I purchased several gowns in the village yesterday, but I find they are in need of altering." She cleared her throat. What had happened to the feelings of superiority she had always felt?

Mrs. Dawson nodded. "That is usually the case when one buys dresses which are already made. Did the shop owner not offer to make the alterations for you?"

Zia's face heated and she nodded. "She did, but only after making several disparaging comments about my ability to pay. My pride would not allow me to spend even another minute in the woman's company." She looked at her feet. "I had thought," she swallowed and took a deep breath, "or rather hoped you might assist me in altering the gowns?"

Zia chanced a glance at the older woman. She stared at Zia with her mouth slightly open and a brow raised. Zia shook her head. "Do not concern yourself. I apologize for intruding upon your sewing time. I shall ask Lucy if she might assist me." She turned on her heel to leave but was stopped before she could clear the sofa table.

"I find I should like that very much." Mrs. Dawson glanced

down at the fabric in her lap. "It hurts when someone treats you as lesser than you are, does it not?"

Zia closed her eyes, biting down hard on the inside of her cheek. In the deepest recesses of her mind—the thoughts she denied but deep, deep down knew to be true—she knew this was the reason she was hesitant to ask Mrs. Dawson for help.

Zia had treated this woman poorly, this woman who had been so kind to take her in. Tiana would have surely been disappointed in Zia. She would have said nothing, but it would have been there, in her eyes. "I do not know what to say, for a simple apology seems woefully inadequate."

Mrs. Dawson shrugged. "Perhaps it would be best if we forget the past and begin anew." She rose and dipped into a slight curtsy. "My lady, it is a pleasure to make your acquaintance."

Zia smiled. Perhaps this woman did not entirely believe Zia a princess, but she was offering an olive branch of sorts. Zia returned the curtsy. "I can assure you, Mrs. Dawson, the pleasure is all mine. But please, call me Zia."

The two smiled at each other for a moment, as if trying to assess what this new agreement meant for each of them.

"I assume you wish to wear one of the new gowns to Morley Park tonight?" Mrs. Dawson dropped her sewing into the basket next to the sofa.

Zia nodded. "I had hoped to, but I do not know if it is possible to have a dress altered so quickly." She glanced at the clock on the mantle. "It would only give us five hours. While I am not a seamstress, I cannot imagine such a thing can be accomplished." She clutched her hands in front of her. "Or so our modiste in Odessa told me."

Mrs. Dawson smiled the first genuine smile Zia had seen since that first day they'd met and patted Zia's hand. "Let us see how the dress fits before we make any decisions." She motioned with her hand toward the door. "But we have little time to lose."

They walked to Zia's chambers to retrieve the boxes holding the dresses. Zia pulled the gowns out one by one.

Mrs. Dawson's eyes lit. "You have very fine tastes, my—Zia. These gowns are lovely."

Zia smiled and reached for the fabric wrapped in brown paper. "I actually bought this for you. I know Mr. Dawson was to buy you fabric to make some dresses, but I thought this looked so happy. It reminded me of you."

Mrs. Dawson tilted her head to the side, a soft smile playing at her lips. "Thank you, Zia. That was very thoughtful of you." She unwrapped the fabric and ran her hands over the soft muslin. "You are right, this is very happy, indeed. I like it very much, but I think it would look much better on you."

Zia's face dropped. Mrs. Dawson did not like the fabric and was only trying to keep Zia from feeling hurt. She bit her lower lip. Why had she thought herself so lofty as to think she knew the likes of this woman?

Mrs. Dawson put a hand on Zia's arm. "If I were several years younger, I should love to have a dress from this. It is quite handsome. But I am a widow and nearly an old woman."

Zia pshed. "You are years from being old, Mrs. Dawson." She glanced at the light pink muslin. "But I can see your point. My reading has led me to think English society is more critical on such things than we are in Russia, at least where matters of propriety and fashion for widows are concerned." She took the fabric from the woman's lap and set it aside. "I shall endeavor to return it. Perhaps the shop owner will allow me to trade it for something more to your liking."

Mrs. Dawson pulled the bolt back onto her lap. "I do not think you should return it. It would make a lovely gown for you." She glanced up at Zia, pausing before continuing on. "We could work on it together, unless you are not inclined to do so. In which case, I am sure the shop would let you exchange it for something else."

Zia smiled. "You would help me to make a dress?" Why did her stomach flutter about at the proposition? Was it not beneath her to make her own clothing?

Perhaps it *was* beneath her, but the bond she felt with Mrs. Dawson right then pushed any thoughts of superiority from her mind. Maybe, just maybe, her time here would not be as lonely as she had feared.

CHAPTER 11

Dawson paced from one end of the entryway to the other waiting for Miss Petrovich and his mother. He pulled the watch from his pocket and checked the time, tapping down his irritation when he realized they had not agreed to meet him for five more minutes.

He was more than grateful to have his mother here at Fawnbrooke. And Miss Petrovich—he had not allowed himself to think overly much on how he felt about her. But it was times such as this that he missed living alone, coming and going as he pleased without waiting for anyone.

A rustling at the top of the stairs drew his attention upward and all irritation and thoughts of being on his own fled from his mind. Miss Petrovich stood in a lovely blue gown he had never seen before.

Dawson swallowed, only then noticing his mother standing just behind the young lady. A smile played at her lips and he was at a loss to know what she found humorous. Putting his finger between his throat and his collar, Dawson gave a small tug, trying to rid himself of the tightness he felt.

The ladies descended the staircase. Miss Petrovich smiled up at him and his face warmed. What was wrong with him? Was he becoming ill? Perhaps he should instruct Mrs. Hardy to use less coal, as the house seemed almost suffocatingly warm tonight. There was no sense wasting good coal when it was not needed.

Lucy came from the small coatroom with her arms loaded down.

Dawson stepped forward and took his greatcoat and hat, trying to relieve the girl of some of the weight.

His mother cleared her throat. "Dugray, does not Zia look lovely tonight?" Her tone held a touch of disapproval. No doubt because she had been forced to make mention of it instead of Dawson commenting of his own accord.

Dawson tugged on his coat, casting a glance over his shoulder, but paused when he looked at her again. Lud, she *was* beautiful tonight. He did not remember seeing another her equal. But it would not be proper to tell her such things. Besides, from all he had learned of the lady, she would not welcome his good opinion should he give it to her. Instead, he offered a small smile. "Yes, Mother, you are quite right. She looks very handsome."

A shadow passed over Miss Petrovich's eyes and her brow furrowed. Was she disappointed in his comment? He shrugged, his own brow furrowing. Perhaps he had been wrong. After all, if she was a princess, would she not expect people to express their admiration for her beauty? And if she were merely a servant, she would likely not be accustomed to comments about her beauty, which would make them that much more welcome, would it not?

Dawson ran a hand through his hair, letting a deep, long sigh whisper from his lips. This was why he enjoyed living alone. He held far fewer expectations of himself than it seemed these ladies did. But there was no fixing it. If he were to make a fuss about her appearance now, it would come across as false and insincere.

Pushing his hat firmly down on his head, Dawson turned to the ladies. Miss Petrovich stood in her serviceable cloak, tugging the ribbons of her bonnet into a tight bow beneath her chin.

His mother laced her fingers together, pushing her fingers into her gloves. She looked up at him.

"Are we ready to depart then?" He looked mostly to his mother because he felt his breath hitch each time he looked at Miss Petrovich.

Miss Petrovich tilted her head slightly to the side before giving him a nod.

"Splendid. Then let us be on our way." He held out a hand, allowing the ladies to precede him from the house. Tad's borrowed carriage waited outside the house; the driver Dawson had hired stood with the horses, talking quietly to them while they waited.

Dawson opened the door and handed his mother up, as he had not the money to hire a footman yet, and he had not seen the need for one. Miss Petrovich placed her hand in his and a warm tingle raced up his arm. He flexed his hand several times, trying to make the tingle go away. Perhaps a footman was more essential than he had originally thought.

"Thank you," she murmured to him as she stepped inside the carriage.

Dawson settled himself on the seat opposite her and his mother. He twisted his head from side to side, but still the tightness remained in his throat. He rapped several times on the side of the carriage, pitching slightly forward as the carriage began to move.

Miss Petrovich was quiet, looking out the window. What she was looking at in the darkness, Dawson could not fathom. Clouds covered the sky, blotting out any moonlight. But apparently complete darkness was of more interest than what was within the carriage.

Dawson glanced at his mother. Her eyes bulged and she nodded toward Miss Petrovich. What did she wish him to do? Engage in meaningless, trivial conversation? She should know him enough to know that was not likely to happen.

He turned his own gaze out the opposite window. His stomach twisted and his muscles felt taut, but at the same time jumpy. He growled low in his throat. *Gah, very well.* "I do not recall seeing that gown among the items we were able to salvage. Did you purchase it in the village?"

Miss Petrovich kept her gaze out the window. Was she ignoring him, or did she not realize he was speaking to her? He was finding addressing her increasingly difficult, as he did not really know *how* to address her. Calling her princess, as he had previously done, seemed unkind because he had only done so with facetiousness. Yet calling her Miss Petrovich to her face also seemed wrong, if indeed she was a princess.

She had said he could call her Lady Zia, but that did not suit her either. The whole situation left him confused and uncertain, neither of which he enjoyed. And yet, he felt at a loss for how to correct the situation.

The carriage stopped and Dawson had never felt so grateful to arrive at Tad's. He nearly leapt from his seat and pushed open the door, breathing in the cold winter air until it brought him a hint of calm.

Tad sat back in his chair, taking a long drink of the claret in his glass. He was seated at the head of the table, with the duchess to one side of him and Dawson to the other. Dawson's mother sat next to him and Miss Petrovich was seated next to the duchess, a notion which both pleased and annoyed Dawson, both for the same reason. Across from him, she was always within view. Had she been placed next to him, he might have felt her presence, but at least he would not have had to look on her for the entirety of the meal.

While Dawson quite enjoyed looking upon her—for what gentleman would not—he disliked the effect it had on him. Several times in the course of the meal he had completely lost his train of thought when he glanced in her direction.

He had noticed Tad grin when he looked between the two of them. No doubt, His Grace believed he had uncovered some great secret. He was wrong, of course, but it still galled Dawson to have Tad thinking he knew something, especially something concerning Dawson and his feelings.

"Dawson?" Tad's voice penetrated Dawson's thoughts.

He sat up straighter, looking at Tad with guilty eyes. Why did he feel as if he were being called to task? He scowled at Tad. "What?"

Tad only grinned in return. Yes, he thought he knew something. "I asked if you thought we might be able to do some work on the tenant cottages this week. The weather has been cold, but the moisture has been low."

Dawson rubbed at his chin. "That is my hope. I believe if we have a solid week of dry, we should be able to repair all of the roofs. Then any repairs to the interiors can be made, no matter the weather."

Tad nodded. "I shall inform my new secretary and have him schedule it in."

Dawson shifted in his seat and ran a hand through his hair.

Tad beamed. "I confess, I find I am highly anticipating the

work. It has been too long since we undertook such a project. Do you not agree?"

"Are you implying you are to do the work yourselves?" Miss Petrovich looked between the two men.

Tad nodded. "And why should we not?"

She gave a small cough. "You are a duke." Her gaze flicked to Dawson. "And you are a gentleman. Is that not work for you to hire someone to do?"

Tad sat up straighter in his chair, his nostrils slightly flared. Dawson had heard this conversation before, and he did not wish to hear it again, especially not directed at Miss Petrovich. He cleared his throat and Tad glanced over. Dawson shook his head and Tad's shoulders relaxed.

Dawson leaned forward. It was remarks such as this that made Dawson question if Miss Petrovich was, indeed, telling them the truth of her title. "We do hire people to help, but we, both of us, find great satisfaction in working with our hands and seeing a job done well."

Miss Petrovich seemed unconvinced.

Tad swallowed the claret and leaned forward. "Miss—my lady." He looked at Dawson for help.

Dawson merely shrugged.

Tad narrowed his eyes a fraction before turning back to Miss Petrovich. "I was not raised to be a duke. There were many in line ahead of me, so the notion never seemed a possibility. I was raised on a large and very profitable estate, but my father insisted my brother and I learn every aspect of the estate. He said one cannot manage property effectively if one does not know what each job involves." He shifted to the side, resting his elbow on the arm of his chair. "It should not matter if I am a duke or simply the owner of a small farm. I should know what needs to be done because I have done it myself before. Besides, how am I to know if the work was done properly, if I know not how to do the work myself?"

Miss Petrovich looked at her plate, pushing a slice of mutton around. "This is not a view the nobility in my country have."

Dawson set his fork onto his plate. "There are many here who hold a similar opinion. I believe if you stay in England long enough, you will find His Grace is not a typical duke."

Miss Petrovich nodded but said nothing more.

Tad leaned against the wall, swirling the dark red liquid in his glass. "I believe your attitude has changed toward your foreign guest."

Dawson scoffed. "You are daft and perhaps could use a pair of spectacles."

Tad laughed quietly. "Tell me, what is it that has changed your mind? Last we spoke of her, you thought her quite a falsifier."

Dawson raised a brow. "I did not say I have altered my opinion of the lady."

"Come now, Dawson. I have known you for the whole of my life. I think I know when a lady has caught your eye."

Dawson barked a laugh. "This coming from the man who resorted to fisticuffs because he believed me in love with Violet? I believe you have lost some credibility when it comes to matters of my heart."

Dawson raised his chin and puffed out his chest when Tad's face colored up.

"Yes, well there were other considerations then," Tad said. "I had many burdens which clouded my judgement. Now I am completely unencumbered and feel nothing for the girl in question, so I am unbiased in my belief of your feelings for her." Tad placed a hand on Dawson's shoulder. "Why are you denying this? I think it the best news I've heard."

Dawson's chin dropped back down, and his body sagged. "If it were true," he said, squinting at Tad, "which I am not saying it is, it is a hopeless situation."

"Why would you say such a thing?"

"Can you not see it? If she is a servant, then she is dishonest. I could never trust her and that is not what I desire in a marriage. If she is telling the truth?" He sighed. "She is so far above my station it is laughable to think we could ever make a go of it." He dropped into a chair. "If she is a princess, she is accustomed to palaces and grand balls, not a manor house in ill repair. I am barely a gentleman, and by some, will never be considered such. I barely have two shillings to rub together. Why should a princess even consider the likes of me?"

Tad sat in the chair opposite Dawson and placed his elbows on his knees. "Because she loves you." Tad leaned forward. "Or she could, in time. I do not think either of you have spent enough time together to know your true inclinations, but I do believe something could happen."

Dawson snorted. "When did you become a matchmaker, Tad?" He shook his head, unable to believe what Tad had said. "Even if it could be true, she would come to resent my low status. And by that time, I am convinced I should be unequivocally in love with her." He slapped his hand on the table. "No. It is not worth it."

CHAPTER 12

Zia pulled the cloak over her shoulders and fastened it with one hand while she retrieved the small bouquet of flowers off the table. The duchess had asked a maid to gather them from the Morley hothouse the previous night. Zia must take a token with her, the duchess had insisted.

Zia tried to swallow past the lump in her throat, the tightness aching all the way to her ears. She had yet to visit Tiana's grave, but she could put it off no longer. Her stomach joined in tormenting her, twisting and turning about. She had known she needed to make this trip, but every time she glanced out her bedroom window she'd been paralyzed with apprehension. As if visiting Tiana's grave would make her death a reality. As it was now, Zia was able to hope someone else was buried beneath that mound of dirt. But for Tiana's sake, Zia could deny it no longer.

She grabbed a rug off the nearby chair and headed for the door. A cold wind blasted her face as she stepped out, almost making her reconsider her decision. Could this visit not wait until another day? Surely, it would warm, and the wind would let up soon. She glanced back at the doorway. It was not as if Tiana was going anywhere.

Zia cringed and her throat tightened even more. How could she think such unkind thoughts? She closed her eyes as tears stung behind her lids. *You can do this, Zia. You must do this.* It was likely the only way to get the nightmares to stop.

A gust of wind passed through her cloak and dress, making her knees knock together. Zia tightened the cloak around her, but it did little good. She longed for the warmth of *her* cloak, but the thought of wearing it made her shudder. Tiana had died in that cloak. Besides, it would do Zia good to feel what Tiana had felt every time they had ventured out into the cold. Did not Zia deserve to suffer? Had she not been the cause of the accident and Tiana's death?

Zia put her head down, watching her feet take one step at a time, occasionally glancing up to check her progress. When she finally saw the church, she could barely feel her toes.

She looked behind her. A trail of smoke curled from the chimneys at the house. Perhaps she'd had the right of it earlier and she should make this journey on a warmer day.

But then the sounds of hammer strikes caught her ear. If Mr. Dawson and the duke could mend rooftops in such weather, she could certainly visit Tiana's grave.

She took a deep breath, rubbing her hands up and down her arms. It provided just enough warmth to convince her to press forward toward the church. She quickened her pace, hoping the exercise would keep her warmer.

There was no headstone yet, and in truth, Zia did not know if there was a plan to ever get one. Perhaps she could arrange for it. It was the least she could do.

Zia stood at the foot of the dirt mound where Tiana lay. Her mind felt completely blank. What did one say to a grave? She had visited her mother's grave often enough, but she mostly just plucked at the grass that surrounded the headstone.

Zia shuffled from one foot to the other, a desire for warmth only part of the reason for the action. Her fingers tightened around the flower stems in her hand and the thorn of a rose penetrated her glove and dug into her flesh. She glanced down at the roses, only now remembering she had brought them with her.

She leaned forward, placing the flowers on the mounded dirt. "These are for you, Tiana. I know how much you love flowers." Zia stood silent for a moment.

Placing the rug to the ground, ensuring it was still folded over several times so as to keep the cold from seeping through, Zia dropped down to her knees on the blanket. Then she lowered her head into her hands. "I am sorry. It was not even my idea to bring the flowers. The Duchess of Shearsby insisted on it." Her brow creased. "What kind of person am I, Tiana? Even now, after putting you in this cold grave, I do not consider you and your wants. Why did you put up with me for so long?"

While no answer came to her question, Zia felt some comfort in speaking her native Russian again. "I am sorry I made us leave the inn. Had I not been so stubborn and insisted we press on, perhaps you would not be in the ground, but here with me instead." Why was she speaking to Tiana, as if she were there and could offer a response? Zia did not know why, but just saying the words out loud lifted some of the burden from her shoulders. "But then I would likely still be the selfish girl you knew." Was it wrong to think that perhaps something good had come from her maid's death?

A chill ran through her body. "Why did you never tell me how little warmth this cloak provided?" She knew the answer before the question had fully left her mouth. "I would not have heard you had you told me, would I? It has never been my way to worry on anyone but myself."

Zia rubbed at her nose with the back of her hand. The cold had made it nearly numb, but still she could feel the warmth of the moisture dripping from it. She didn't know if it was her emotions or the cold making every orifice on her face leak today.

"I am unsure what you know of the events that have transpired." Could Tiana see her now? Did she know what had happened to them and where they were now? "A gentleman and his mother found us after the accident. He brought us, both of us, back to his estate. You are in a churchyard, if you did not already know such things."

Zia realized she knew little about what happened to a person when they left this world. Had she ever learned of it from any of the sermons in church? She shook the thoughts from her mind. This was not the time to think on such things. She came to... do what? Reconcile with Tiana? Sooth her own conscience?

"I believe you would think Mr. Dawson handsome, but quite dissolute, Tiana. He is all brooding and gruffness, not the kind of gentleman you usually guide me toward. But I find I would have to disagree with you. He is nothing like my father or Prince Sokolov. I have watched him with his mother. To her, he is all kindness. Indeed, do not misunderstand me. He has never treated me cruelly, which I cannot boast of father or Sokolov. I think perhaps he is only suspicious of me. He is never unkind."

Zia thought back on the previous day and their interaction when he gave her the books. A warmth she had not felt before coming to Fawnbrooke settled over her. "I confess, I feel safe with him. Safer than I have ever felt in my life."

The confession took her by surprise. Not because she had said the words aloud, but because she had not realized it to be true. But as she thought on it, she could not deny it. There was something about Mr. Dawson that made her feel at ease, though perhaps ease was not the right word. Mere thoughts of him made her stomach feel restless and her heart never seemed to beat quite right.

Safe was the more accurate word. While she felt he was often put out with her, she also was quite confident that if Prince Sokolov came to take her away, Mr. Dawson would not allow it, unless it was what Zia wished.

She sighed and twisted at the button on her glove sitting at her wrist. "I do not believe he is altogether happy to have me as his guest, but I believe he may be learning to tolerate, perhaps even like my company."

She smiled. "He purchased several gothic novels because I had expressed a desire to read them. He says they are only intended to make his library more diverse, but he allowed me to read them first. I think that may indicate some partiality on his part, does it not?" She looked up when she heard no reply and remembered anew that her friend could not answer.

Zia sighed. Oh, how she wished Tiana could reply. Since the death of Zia's mother, Tiana had been the one to listen to her and offer advice. While Tiana had little experience with love, she was a good listening ear and a sound thinker. She had never lead Zia astray. Indeed, she had warned Zia against the hasty decision to flee Odessa. But Zia had paid her no heed. Another lump formed in Zia's throat, but she pushed her self-loathing thoughts away, if only for a time.

"If there is partiality, it will not last for long, I am sure. Not once he realizes I have lied to him, although, not in the way he believes. I told him I have sent a letter to my uncle, to inform him where I am. But I have not done so yet."

She picked up a pebble from the mound of dirt and rolled it between her thumb and forefinger. "I know what you are thinking. That seeing my uncle was the intention of our visit. But after speaking with Mr. Dawson's neighbor, the Duke of Shearsby, I find myself more cautious than before to make my presence known. The duke did not say it outright, but I think he believes my uncle will return me to Odessa. Or, at the very least, inform my father of where I am. What am I to do, Tiana?"

As the days drew on and there was no word from her uncle, she knew she was only making her position with Mr. Dawson worse. It would not be long now before he realized she had not sent the letter as she had led him to believe. And then what? Would he toss her from his estate? Perhaps Mr. Dawson would deliver her to her uncle, himself, just to be rid of her. The thought unsettled her and not only because of what her uncle might do.

Zia would miss Fawnbrooke. Yes, it was the estate she was coming to cherish. Not because it was grand or lavish, but because of the feelings it drew out in her.

The sewing lessons she had been having with Mrs. Dawson were a pleasant diversion and Zia thought the woman may be warming to her. Their conversations had taken on an informal feel, one that brought with it a feeling of serenity. It reminded Zia of the times she had spent with her mother, though they had never done such menial tasks as sewing clothes. But the interactions felt similar. At first Zia had felt pangs of longing for her mother, but before long they had subsided.

"I wish you were here to tell me what I am to do, Tiana. I have made a muddle of things. The longer I wait to set things to rights, the more I risk losing. But I am frightened of my uncle. What if he sends me back or even worse, uses me for his own benefit? While I am in England, he is my guardian." This was a new thought to Zia. She may very well have removed herself from one precarious situation, only to land herself into another equally as bad.

"I cannot stay here forever, pretending that my uncle has received the letter I have not written and chooses not to come for me." At some point, Mr. Dawson will send inquiries himself, if he hasn't already." She dropped her elbows to her thighs, resting her head in her hands. "Oh, why did I not tell Mr. Dawson the truth from the beginning? What would you have me do?"

A twig snapped behind her and Zia jerked up, looking wildly around her. Mr. Dawson walked several rods away, his head down and his body curled against the cold.

She took a calming breath. There was a chance he had heard her speaking, but it seemed unlikely he could understand Russian, so she need not worry over whether or not he had heard.

Zia put her hands forward and pushed herself to standing. Her feet had not totally lost feeling, as hundreds of pin pricks poked at the soles of her feet. She wiggled her toes and shook each foot in front of her, trying to get the blood circulating into them again.

"I should return to the house. I believe it is getting colder." She gathered the rug and paused. "Rest well, Tiana, my dear friend."

Turning back to the path, Zia made her way to the house and the warmth she needed. Her thoughts turned to the last question she had put to Tiana. What to do about the letter?

Zia did not need Tiana there to tell her what to do. She already knew how the woman would advise her. Make things right by either confessing to Mr. Dawson her deceit or writing the letter to her uncle.

CHAPTER 13

Dawson slammed the door of his study closed behind him. His hands shook, as did his muscles. Whether from anger, exertion, or the cold, he was not sure. But why was he so angry by what he had heard Miss Petrovich speak of in the churchyard? Had he not known all along she was not being honest with him? So why was hearing it from her own lips making him so angry?

He walked over to the fireplace and grabbed the poker from the tools leaned up against the wall. Poking and stirring the fire, he wondered if the anger was directed toward Miss Petrovich or himself. Why should he be mad at her for confirming his suspicions?

In truth, he was angry at himself for letting her get to him. He had felt himself softening toward her the more time he spent with her. He had allowed himself to use small things to convince him that he had been mistaken—that he had misjudged her.

He tossed some coal on the fire with a grunt. But was this not what he had been hoping all along? That she was not, indeed, a princess? He had been denying his attraction to her. Even telling himself it was not real. But the fact remained, if she was a princess, there was not a chance that any attachment could form between them. The disparity between their stations would be so great that he had not a hope of securing her hand.

But hearing the truth had not brought the relief he thought it would. Perhaps it was because she had not told him of her deceit but rather, he had overheard her confessing her sins to a mound of dirt in the churchyard. Why would she not just come and tell him the truth? Face to face with her own words?

She had turned and seen him there on the path, but he doubted she realized he was close enough to hear, nor that he understood Russian. Or, at least enough Russian to decipher what she had been telling her dead friend, or mistress, or whoever it was lying buried there.

Once he had heard her ask why she had not told him the truth from the beginning, he had ducked his head and walked quickly away. What would he have said to her had he stayed? It felt wrong to confront her with her lies there in the churchyard. He did not believe that the spirits of those buried there, if there even were spirits at all, would care. But something had still felt improper about confronting her just then.

Besides, Dawson had learned that it was best if he was able to organize his thoughts before approaching people on matters such as this. He did not do well speaking extemporaneously, with only emotions driving him.

He dropped into a chair and stretched his legs out in front of him, crossing them at his ankles. Why was Miss Petrovich out in the cold in that terrible cloak? It could not possibly provide the warmth one needed to be kneeling, for who knows how long, on the cold ground. Why would she not wear the heavy one William had retrieved from the carriage? Was it simply a matter that she could not wear something that was not hers?

Dawson snorted. Perhaps she would only allow herself to assume titles which were not her own, but her sensibilities would not allow her to wear her mistress's clothes.

Or perhaps she could not wear it because she knew a person had died while wearing it. He had to admit, the notion did feel a bit ghoulish. But could she not overlook the eeriness for the warmth that was surely needed when out of doors in this weather? He believed he could, if in the same situation, but in truth, he did not know. He had never been in the position of having to actually decide such a thing.

He rubbed at his cold chin. If the cloak was put to pieces and the fur transferred to a different cloak, would Miss Petrovich have a change of heart? Dawson shook his head. What was he thinking? Was he not angry at the woman? Why was he even considering making a trip to the village to have a new cloak made for her? He gave the fire another swift stir. But then, providing the woman with warmth was not showing her any partiality. It was simply providing for her welfare. It was something anyone calling himself a gentleman would do, was it not?

He had no plans this afternoon. He could take the cloak to the seamstress this very day. His chest tightened. But would any gentleman make a special trip into the village just for the cloak of a woman he had no feelings nor inclinations toward?

Dawson grunted then snapped his fingers. While he was in the village, he could make arrangements for the supplies he needed for the next phase of repairs on the tenant cottages. That was truly the reason for his trip. He would simply see to the cloak while he was already in the village on other matters of business. Yes, that was the right of it. He was not paying Miss Petrovich any special attentions.

Perhaps he would stop in at Morley Park on his way back. He and Tad could make the plans for the remaining repairs on the cottages, based on the information Dawson gathered when arranging for the supplies. Besides, Tad would surely have a better perspective on what Dawson had just learned of Miss Petrovich and her dishonesty. Even if Tad did not have any insight, it would be a way for Dawson to give voice to his thoughts before he approached Miss Petrovich.

He gave his head a firm nod. He would have Lucy retrieve the cloak from Miss Petrovich's chambers and then he would take it into the village this afternoon.

Dawson moved to the corner and pulled the bell, then returned to the fire. He put his hands out, warming them through before he journeyed out into the cold again.

Dawson walked out of the dressmaker's shop, a satisfied smile on his lips. She had promised to have the cloak finished by tomorrow next. It was faster than Dawson had thought possible.

The woman treated the cloak with near reverence when she saw it. Dawson had known it was of fine quality, but he had not known just how fine. The fur, according to Mrs. Partridge, was rare and very expensive. The expense of the new wool it would take to replace the old was more than Dawson had thought to spend, but in the end, Mrs. Partridge had lowered the price as she said she could use the original wool for another cloak.

A lightness settled over him. He was pleased to have been able to provide this kindness for Miss Petrovich. He mounted his horse and set out for the duke's estate.

The ride to Morley felt shorter than his trip into the village, but Dawson did not take the time to evaluate the reason. Dismounting, he handed the reins over to the stable boy.

"Afternoon, Mr. Dawson."

Dawson grinned down at the boy. "Good afternoon, Charlie."

The boy rubbed the nose of Dawson's mount, Ares. "I sure have missed him, sir." He slipped an apple from his pocket and allowed the horse to lip it from the palm of his hand.

Dawson chuckled. "And he has missed you, Charlie. Of that I can assure you. No one takes such good care of him."

Charlie ducked his head in embarrassment.

"I am certain you will make a very competent stable master someday." Dawson rumpled the boy's hair before turning and heading for the house.

He entered the house when Baker opened the door, stopping in the grand entryway. It was curious. Dawson had lived in this house for more than two years, and yet it still did not have the feeling of home that he already felt at Fawnbrooke.

But then, Morley was not his, as was Fawnbrooke. And Miss Petrovich and his mother did not wait for him at Morley.

Dawson frowned.

Miss Petrovich?

He did not like the path of his thoughts. It was his mother which made Fawnbrooke feel like home. Miss Petrovich was merely a guest.

"Dawson, I did not expect to see you this afternoon." Tad's voice boomed from the upper landing, echoing through the entryway.

Dawson raised a hand in greeting. "I apologize for not sending word of my coming, but I was in the village and I thought to stop by and speak with you on my way home."

Tad waved him up the stairs. "No apology needed. Come, let us retire to my study to talk."

Dawson mounted the stairs, two at a time, neither man speaking as they walked down the corridor.

Tad pushed through the door to his study and Dawson took in the familiarity of it, the dark woods and fabrics making the room feel warm and comforting. The smell of leather and wood polish mixed with sandalwood was a scent that was wholly Tad. Dawson had spent most of his two years at Morley Park in this very room. He hoped one day to have a study that brought this same feeling in his own home. As it was, his makeshift study was dingy and small.

Tad sat down behind his desk and glanced over at the young man sitting at a table in the corner. "If you would please take that work and finish it at your desk, Stanton." Tad looked back at Dawson with a single brow raised.

Stanton stuttered out a response as he messily gathered the papers into his arms and headed for the door which lead into the secretary's small office. A few papers fluttered from his arms as he twisted the knob on the door. Rather than bend down and pick them up, he scooted the papers through the doorway with his foot.

When the door was firmly closed, Dawson looked over at Tad with a grin.

"Perhaps it is fortuitous that you stopped by. I am hopeful you can help me decipher what all of these piles mean." He motioned to several stacks of papers on his desk. "It seems my new secretary has a different way of organizing than you did. I am not yet accustomed to it."

Dawson laughed. "I will see what I can do."

"Very good." Tad sighed. "That is not why you stopped to speak with me, however. What were you doing in the village?"

"I was arranging for the supplies—" Dawson slapped a hand to his forehead. "Hounds an' tares. I forgot to stop in at Mr. Lundy's shop." He rubbed his thumb and forefinger over both of his eyes. Was that not the whole reason for his trip into the village?

Tad cleared his throat. "If that was the reason for your trip, how did you forget to stop there?" His brow was creased in confusion.

Dawson pushed a breath out slowly through his teeth. "I made another stop first."

Tad looked at him, his lips already beginning to turn up at the corners. "And what was this stop that made it impossible for you to remember anything else? It would not have been the bookshop for more gothic novels, would it?"

Dawson scowled at Tad. "No. It was not the bookshop. And why should you speak as if my buying such books was about anything other than building my library? Does not your library have gothic novels?"

Tad nodded. "Yes, indeed; you are correct. What was it then that caused you to forget Mr. Lundy?"

Dawson sunk deeper in his seat. Tad already had it in his mind that Dawson's lapse in memory was due to Miss Petrovich. Telling him of the stop at the dress shop would only affirm his notions, as misguided as they were. "I do not see how that is relevant information. And my forgetfulness does not prohibit us from discussing the plans for the interior of the cottages."

Tad grinned fully. "No. You are right, *it* does not prohibit the discussion, but *I* might. I do not believe I shall be able to concentrate on anything else until my curiosity has been assuaged."

Dawson ran a hand over the back of his neck, kneading at the muscles there. "Must you be like this?"

Tad nodded thoughtfully. "I am afraid I must. For I believe it must surely have something to do with Miss Petrovich, or whatever she is calling herself these days. And I wish to hear you say you have more than a mild interest in her."

Dawson growled, which only seemed to confirm to Tad that he

was correct. "Some days, Tad, I wonder why we have stayed friends for so long. You are an infuriating man."

"Only when you know I am right." He leaned back in his chair, steepling his fingers. It was a sure sign Dawson would get no planning done until he gave Tad what he wanted. Sometimes, dealing with Tad was like dealing with a child.

He stared at the large red poppy flower woven into the rug. "If you must know, I made a stop at the dress shop."

Tad's brows quirked. "Buying the lady gowns? This has progressed further than I thought."

"I bought nothing of the sort," Dawson snapped. "William retrieved a fur-lined cloak from the carriage when we rescued Miss Petrovich. It is a warm cloak, yet she has refused to wear it, I can only assume because of the memories attached to it. Instead, she wears a flimsy thing which cannot possibly provide her any warmth. I thought if the fur cloak was remade, with a different color of wool, perhaps she might be able to see it not as the one her mistress was wearing when she died, but as something new."

Dawson looked up at Tad, expecting a huge smile to cover his face. A smile was there, but it was softer, with less of a gloat to it. "That was very gentlemanly of you, Dawson." He leaned forward. "If this is what you do for someone you care little for, I can only guess what you would do for one you *truly* care for."

Dawson looked away, his skin feeling hot and sweaty. "Now that I told you, may we discuss what I came to speak with you about?" He knew when he brought up Miss Petrovich and what he had overheard, it would start Tad gloating all over again. But he needed Tad's advice, so he took a deep breath and nearly plunged ahead. But then Zia's face flashed into his mind and again, his face flushed with heat.

Perhaps he would start the discussion on the tenant cottages first.

CHAPTER 14

Dark brown eyes leaned in, never leaving Zia's. He was going to kiss her. Her heart thundered in her ears and heat rushed to every point in her body. She felt his breath on her cheek and her eyes fluttered closed as she waited to feel his lips on hers. She raised a hand, expecting to feel the beard beneath her fingers. But it was not there, only cleanly shaven skin.

Zia bolted upright and threw back the covers. Her eyes slowly adjusting to the dark. She threw her feet over the side of the bed and dropped them to the cold floorboards. The nightmares had decreased since visiting Tiana's grave a few days prior but having Mr. Dawson replace Tiana was unexpected, albeit not wholly unpleasant.

Zia stood up, but then sank back onto her bed, willing her pulse to slow. This was the first time she had recognized the eyes of the bearded man from her dreams when she had first arrived at Fawnbrooke. Mr. Dawson's eyes. How had she never realized they were one and the same before?

She had run into the bearded man at the inn, before the accident. It was a wonder after that interaction that he had stopped to help her at all. It also explained why he thought her lying about her title. She had not thought Tiana played the role of a lady very convincingly. But perhaps Zia had been wrong. It was yet another element of her plan that had so fully gone awry.

She pushed back the stray hairs that fell onto her cheeks from her plait. Her face warmed as she thought on the dream she had just awoken from. Mr. Dawson had been leaning in, his purpose no doubt to kiss her, when something had awakened her. She was both disappointed and relieved. How was she to look at Mr. Dawson had she actually allowed the dream kiss to happen? Judging from her rapid pulse and heated flesh, she would surely have let it happen. *In her dreams*, she reminded herself. It was only a figment of her imagination.

Mr. Dawson had never indicated, nor done anything remotely close to those things he had done in her dreams, which meant it was only her feeling these emotions. He had not even thought her handsome the night they went for dinner at Morley Park.

She ran her fingers over her lips, the tingle of anticipation still there. If only something had not awakened her, she would know what it felt like. But what had awakened her? Was it only the recognition of Mr. Dawson's deep brown eyes? She grabbed her wrap from the nearby chair and slid her arms through, tying it tightly at her waist.

She walked lightly to her door, listening to see if she could hear anything on the other side. Footsteps sounded, but they were farther away, perhaps downstairs even. Should she light a candle? She looked toward the bedside table, but quickly dismissed the notion. Her eyes had fully adjusted to the darkness.

Placing a hand on the door and the casing, she turned the knob with the other hand, hoping to keep the door from making any sound. Most of the squeaky hinges had been dealt with over the last few days, but every now and again, one would make itself known. She hoped this early morning hour would not be this door's turn. It came open without a sound and Zia closed her eyes in a brief prayer of thanks.

She tiptoed into the corridor, training her ears to the sounds of the house and those that were foreign. She again heard footsteps below followed by a few gruff, whispered voices. Suddenly her hands felt very empty. She had no notion of who was below. What if there was an intruder? Why had she not grabbed something to defend herself?

A small table sat in an alcove just ahead. The candelabra on the table could surely be of use. She snatched it up on her way by and continued down the stairs.

A dark figure stood to the side of the doorway, staring out into the night through the sidelights. He was tall and broad, not unlike Mr. Dawson, although this man seemed to slouch a bit more. He took a deep breath, his shoulders rising and falling. What was he waiting for? More men to join him?

Zia walked quietly until she was only a few steps behind him. She raised her weapon over her head and began its downward trajectory, just as the man turned around. Mr. Dawson's eyes widened when he saw the candleholder flashing toward him. His hand shot out, grasping Zia's wrist and bringing the candelabra to a stop.

Her wrist burned with his touch and she released the weapon. It clattered to the floor.

He pulled her gently toward him and whispered, "Are you trying to awaken the entire household, Princess?"

She shook her head, suddenly aware of how close they were. The tingle in her lips returned and she bit the inside of her cheek to keep herself from running her tongue over them.

His gaze dropped to her lips and he sighed. She felt the breath on her cheek and her own breath shuddered out of her.

Mr. Dawson dropped her wrist and took a step back into the darkness. "What are you doing up, Princess?"

"I have asked you not to call me that." Her voice was quiet and shy.

"I believe you only asked for me not to use that tone." He looked down at her, but his face was shadowed by the night. "I thought my tone had changed. Does it still bother you, Princess?"

If he talked to her like this, she thought he could call her anything he wished. She swallowed, glad he could not see the color that was surely tinting her cheeks and ears. It was, no doubt, even down her neck. "You could just call me Zia."

"But what if I like princess better?" He took a step closer.

She stared up at him, sure that if she spoke now, he would know all of her feelings. Oh, why had she had that dream?

"Well?"

"You may call me Zia. But I find that I do not mind princess so much anymore."

He smiled—genuinely smiled—at her. She reached out and grasped hold of his arm, desperately in need of support.

"Very well, Princess. What are you doing up at this hour?" He placed both his hands on her upper arms, as if he were afraid she might lose her balance again.

"I heard a sound and it awakened me. I came to see what it was." She sounded breathless.

He was close enough now that she could see the grin on his face and the slight wrinkles to the sides of his eyes. Oh, that was not good. She yearned to reach out and touch those wrinkles. Instead, she clasped her hands tightly in front of her.

"I am sorry I awakened you." He sheepishly dropped his hands from her arms and looked down at the floor. "The lid of my trunk slipped from my hand." He reached over and grabbed his hat from the side table.

"Your trunk?" Only then did she realize he was dressed in his great coat, his hat turning in his hands. "Where are you going in the middle of the night?"

He looked at her for a moment, his gaze dropping to her wrap and he cleared his throat. "Tad and I are for Northamptonshire to visit the Earl of Somerton. He has a horse I should like to purchase." He glanced out the window. A faint pink outlined the hills on the horizon. "The weather has been holding the past few days. We are hoping it will continue a few days more."

Zia's shoulders sagged. Had she not heard him, he would have left without even saying goodbye.

Did his mother know? She had made no mention of it. She shook her head. Silly girl. Of course his mother knew. Zia took a step back, needing the control that the added distance between them gave her. "You were going to leave without saying goodbye?" Why did she feel he must inform her of his comings and goings? It was not as if she had any hold on him. She was only a guest in his house, after all.

"I did not realize you wished me to offer my farewells." He turned the hat in his hands over again. "My apologies, Princess." He was correct. His tone had most definitely changed. This new one nearly melted her to the bone.

Zia thought she saw him frown, but perhaps it was just the shadows. "When I return, I shall see you are delivered to your uncle's estate. Your letters must have gone awry. It is the only explanation as to why he has not come for you, or at least sent a letter in response."

It was not just shadows then. "Whatever you think is best, sir." Her chest felt tight and she thought she may not be able to take a full breath. He wished her away from Fawnbrooke.

The sound of horse hooves outside turned his attention away from her. He moved toward the door but turned back to her. "I am glad you are to be here with my mother. I worried about her staying on here by herself, but with you here, I shall not worry. Thank you for that."

As if I had a choice. That must be the reason he was waiting until he got back to take her to her uncle's, for it was clearly evident he was ready to be rid of her.

He opened the door and stepped out onto the terrace but turned back to her again. His mouth opened but then he closed it. He gave Zia a long look, then shook his head and shut the door behind him.

Zia stared out the window of the parlor. The ground was devoid of snow, but the cold was obvious as the wind blew leaves in circular patterns on the ground. She shuddered involuntarily.

The house was warm enough, with ample fires stoked and burning. But something was missing. *He* was missing.

Zia scowled, the frown reflecting back at her in the glass. Why should she feel so morose just because Mr. Dawson was gone? Was it not only a matter of days before she would be the one leaving? Had he not told her that when he returned, he would take her to see her uncle—*because surely her letters had gone awry*—for that seemed the only reason he had not yet come for her, or even written a response? The doubt in his voice still echoed in her mind. Oh, those dratted letters!

In a moment of weakness, she had told him she had written to her uncle yet again. Why did she continue to perpetuate the first lie?

Even worse, why did she continue to dream of him? Only now,

instead of a noise waking her up, the dream continued on. Mr. Dawson would bend to kiss her, and her eyes would flutter shut. But instead of feeling his lips on hers, she would wait for something that never came. When she opened her eyes, he would be smirking at her. "Do you really think I could love a pseudologist?" Then he would laugh at her. His laughter was what woke her from the dream every night.

Mr. Dawson had said he was relieved that she was to be here while he and the duke traveled to Northamptonshire, but she found it difficult to find any hope that his affections could turn toward her from those few words.

Her throat squeezed and it felt as if food had become lodged inside. The edges of her sight blurred, and she rubbed an angry hand across her eyes. Why did she care if he did not want her here? He was an angry, gruff man and she did not need his kind.

In truth, she was angrier at herself. This was not her. She had never worried after the good opinion of a person so decidedly below her station. And yet, those words brought more tears to her eyes. She was just being a stupid girl.

"Zia, dear?" Mrs. Dawson spoke from the doorway and Zia quickly blinked any remaining tears away and pretended to focus on the book in her lap.

"Yes? Are you in need of my help, Mrs. Dawson?" She was grateful she had insisted the woman call her by her Christian name days earlier. Much of the earlier awkwardness that her title seemed to cause had dissipated as she and Mrs. Dawson had spent more and more time together.

"I am not in need of you, if you are engrossed in your book, dear. I only thought to start work on your gown. But it can wait for another day."

Zia tossed her book to the side and hopped off the bench. "No. I am not so engrossed as to pass up your offer. I should love to start on it. I have never seen the process of making clothing before."

Mrs. Dawson clasped her hands in front of her chest. "Then let us get started. I do not believe we can have the gown done before Dugray returns, but if we get started right away, we might come close."

Zia nodded, a smile playing at the corners of her mouth. While the woman never came out and suggested a match between Zia and her son, there were subtle inferences made. Zia's brows crinkled in thought. Or that was what Zia believed. Could she be wrong? Could the inference that the dress may be close to completion before Mr. Dawson returned mean something different than Zia believed? Mrs. Dawson was surely implying that it would be nearly complete before Mr. Dawson was to take her to Chatney House.

She rotated her shoulders and stretched, following Mrs. Dawson down the corridor. Why did she over think everything these days? It seemed as though she could not have a single thought without turning it over and over in her mind. It was taxing, and she was thoroughly sick of it.

She made up her mind right then. Today would be about enjoying her time with Mrs. Dawson and that was all. She would not allow herself to think about or analyze anything more. Especially concerning Mr. Dawson.

CHAPTER 15

Dawson slowed Ares, slumping forward slightly as Fawnbrooke came into view. The aches and cold he had been pushing off descended on him, making him question if he could make it the last thirty rods to the house before exhaustion overtook him. Ares seemed to take the final steps of the journey without any help from Dawson.

David Preston dismounted next to him and stood, waiting for Dawson to do the same. "I will see to the horses, sir."

Dawson gave the young man a nod and slipped off his saddle. "Thank you, David. Give them a quick rub down and then get yourself warmed up and find some food." Dawson pulled his great coat a little tighter. "We can finish currying them together." David was one of the few servants that had not come from Morley Park. Dawson had met him just after arriving in England. He had been a stable boy at one of the changing stables in Staffordshire. The two of them had corresponded several times over the last two years.

Dawson had made a point to stop by the changing stables on his way home from Liverpool, hiring David on the spot as his stable master. He was young, not more than two and twenty, but he had a way with horses. Dawson had seen it immediately in their brief encounter two years before. He was just what Dawson needed—someone with natural abilities that Dawson could train and teach after his own ways. There would be no need to undo any poor training from previous teachers. Together they would make a success of the breeding plan for Fawnbrooke.

"Yes, sir." David led the horses toward the barn.

Dawson watched him go, a small smile turning the corners of his lips. Tomorrow, this barn would be home to several horses. A tingle of excitement fluttered in Dawson's stomach. It had come at a greater expense than he had wished but getting the only offspring of the Earl of Somerton's stallion—the legendary *Eclipse* —was well worth the price.

Dawson grunted.

Tad had presented Dawson with many lofty plans, but could this one actually be coming to fruition? It seemed too much to believe. Life had not seemed to work out to his advantage for nigh unto a decade. He had come to think a pleasant sort of life was not what God had in store for him. As he watched David walk the horses back into the stable, he thought perhaps God was finally smiling down on him after all.

He rotated his shoulders and turned toward the house. Any remnants of his smile dropped completely from his face. He had no notion what he would find inside after being gone for nearly week. Had Miss Petrovich finally posted a letter to her uncle by now? Was it possible he had come to fetch her while Dawson was away?

The earlier tingle in his stomach turned sour. Why should he mourn her loss? She had done nothing but falsify everything about herself. It seemed more likely that she had still not sent the letter, because the Duke of Heathrough was not actually her uncle. But how long did she think she could carry on this charade?

Dawson stepped up to the front door and looked down at his mud splattered pants and greatcoat. Mrs. Hardy would surely ring a peal over him for tracking dirt into the house. He glanced longingly at the front door, but instead turned and followed the little path around to the side door. He would use the servants' staircase to his chambers, and perhaps he could be cleaned and presentable before his arrival was discovered.

He stopped inside the doorway, the feeling of home settling on him. He was still in awe of it, even after mere weeks of calling Fawnbrooke home.

At the top of the stairs, he moved lightly toward his chambers at the end of the corridor. But his feet, almost of their own accord, stopped in front of the room occupied by Miss Petrovich. He had not received word from anyone while he had been away, leaving him wondering after her. He raised his hand to knock on her door, but then dropped it. He could squelch his curiosity a while longer and learn of her whereabouts once he was presentable.

He rubbed at his eyes, the burning behind his lids bringing moisture to the corners. A bath would do wonders, but a good night's sleep was what he was in greatest need of. But that would have to wait.

He stepped into the parlor, feeling better after a warm soak than he had thought possible. Even his eyes seemed to burn less than they had before. His gaze immediately turned toward the window seat that Miss Petrovich seemed to prefer. The bench was empty, and Dawson's shoulders dropped a fraction. He scratched at his neck and earlobe. Had she left? Was she even now at Chatney House with her uncle? A hollowness settled in his chest.

He turned his attention to the sofa and was rewarded to see his mother and Miss Petrovich sitting next to each other, deep in a conversation, their heads bent low over something in their laps.

His breath came out in a whoosh. Zia's uncle had not yet come to fetch her. Why did that make him happy?

"Good morning, Mother."

Both women flinched and turned to look at him with slightly widened eyes.

"Good morning, Princess." His voice hitched when Miss Petrovich's head tilted and her lips curved upward.

His mother was the one to speak. "Dugray. You are home." She stood and came toward him, her arms extended. "I see your valet was unable to attend to you while on this trip?" She gave his beard a light tug, but there was a twinkle in her eye.

Dawson raised his shoulders nearly up to his ears, feeling very much like a little boy again. He stepped in and embraced her, relishing in the notion that she was here. It still felt like a dream at times. It had been a long time since he felt someone cared if he returned or not. Not that Tad had not cared, but it was different with his mother.

And Miss Petrovich was different even still. She walked toward him slowly, her hands clasped in front of her. "I hope your trip was successful, sir."

Dawson nodded, his eyes darting around the room. She seemed pleased to see him. His pulse quickened even as his brow furrowed. Why was he frowning? Had he not felt relief when he learned she was still about? He ran a hand across the back of his neck, bringing his shoulders upward at the same time.

The smile dropped from Zia's face and she took several steps back. Her bottom lip turned white as she appeared to bite down hard on it.

Dawson growled low in his throat.

She released her lip and dipped a curtsy. "I am sure you have much to discuss with your mother. I shall give you your privacy."

"You need not leave, child." His mother put a hand on her arm.

Dawson's brow hitched up. What had happened between these two ladies? Their interaction seemed much more familiar than when he had left. In point of fact, he had thought his mother had found Miss Petrovich a bit distasteful. What had happened to bring on this newfound friendship?

Miss Petrovich patted his mother's hand. "Not to worry, Mother D."

Dawson's eyes widened. Tad and his siblings were the only people he knew to call his mother by that name. Even the duchess had not taken to the name, preferring to still call her Mrs. Dawson.

"I find I am in need of some exercise. I have been stooped over my sewing for far too long." Miss Petrovich smiled. "Enjoy some time with your son. I am sure there is much he wishes to tell you." She glanced at the couch. "We can continue our sewing after tea."

Dawson's mother nodded her head. "Do not go far. It is cold out today."

Miss Petrovich nodded. "I will bundle up, I promise." She gave Dawson's mother's hand a quick squeeze and then slipped from the room.

Dawson looked at his mother expectantly. "You seem to have come to an agreement of sorts."

She shrugged. "She is actually a dear, once you spend some time with her. She misses her mother and I believe I fill some of that longing. We have become quite close this last week."

Dawson nodded. "I am glad for it." Was he really? What good would it do for his mother to grow attached to a woman who would, in all likelihood, be leaving before the week's end? Surely, it would not be much longer before Miss Petrovich realized she either had to reveal the truth or leave.

"Do you think it wise to develop such an affinity for her, Mother? Especially considering that she has been less than honest with us?"

His mother led him over to the couch. "I do not believe she has lied to us about her station, Son. I believe it likely she is a princess."

Dawson opened his mouth to refute the assertion, but his mother continued talking.

"I have heard her stories. And she does not speak as a commoner. There is a refinement in her that I believe could only come from years of training."

Dawson let out a heavy sigh. "But Mother, I heard her myself in the churchyard. She admitted to fabling to us." He ran his hands down his thighs. "Everything she has told us may not be a bouncer, but she is hiding something. Of that I am certain."

His mother pulled absently at her mob cap. "Are we all not hiding something, Dugray? Have we not told our share of stories?"

He leaned forward and placed his elbows on his knees. "She knows I am from America."

His mother tsked. "But did you not also tell her we lived in the West Indies?"

Dawson grunted and sat back again. His leg began to bounce lightly. "It is different, Mother. I have to protect Tad and his secret. If word got out that he is from America, he could lose everything. His family, his title. The estate. Everything. I will not have it be me that causes that to happen. He is the closest thing I have to a brother."

His mother placed a hand on his leg, stilling its movement. "I understand, Son. I would not wish to hurt Tad either. All I mean to say is, do not judge Zia on a few lies she may have spun. You know not her reasons for doing so."

Dawson squirmed.

The door opened and Mrs. Hardy walked in. "His Grace is here to see you, sir. I have put him in your study. A parcel arrived for you while you were gone. It is from Mrs. Partridge. I placed that in your study as well."

Dawson blew out a breath and pushed himself to standing. Dawson dropped a kiss on his mother's cheek. "If he is come so soon after returning, it must be important. I should not keep him waiting."

His mother gave him a knowing look. "Make sure to thank Tad for saving you from further conversation on this matter, Son."

Dawson grinned. "I will, indeed." He walked quickly toward the door but stopped just shy of the corridor. He turned back. "I am glad you have come to England, Mother."

"As am I, Dugray."

Dawson moved with purpose to his study. Tad sat in his usual chair across from Dawson's desk.

"I did not expect to see you until tomorrow at the earliest. Has something happened with the horses?"

"To my knowledge, they are proceeding as expected." The duke tossed a paper on the desk. "This was waiting for me when I returned home. It came two days past."

Dawson moved behind his desk and dropped down into his chair. Grabbing his spectacles, he pushed them onto his nose and picked up the paper, reading quickly. He reached the bottom and started over, reading slower. His heart pounded against his ribcage. "She really is a princess."

Tad nodded. "Heathrough seems to believe your guest is his niece."

Dawson squinted at the paper. "But he cannot know for sure which one survived. So it is still possible she is not the princess, just as we originally guessed."

"Yes, it is possible. I did not inform the duke of the demise of the other. But I would guess we will know the truth before the day is out tomorrow. I should expect the duke to descend upon Morley at any time. Violet has the staff preparing rooms for the duke and his party." Tad raised a knowing eyebrow. "You do not look relieved at the prospect of being rid of her."

Dawson grunted. "Do not try and decipher information that is not your business. I shall be perfectly content to have her quit my house. It is my mother I am concerned for. She seems to have developed quite a fondness for the lady while I was gone."

Tad grinned. "Yes, I am sure you are only concerned for Mother D."

Dawson looked at his friend with wide eyes. "Miss Petrovich has begun calling my mother by that name."

Tad scrunched up his nose. "What name? Mother D?" His brows rose when Dawson nodded. "Well, that is something new."

Dawson ran a hand over his face. "Do you think Henderson and the horse carrier will be here before end of day tomorrow?"

Tad stared at him hard before nodding his head. "That was the plan. I trust Henderson to get the horses here as quickly and safely as possible."

Dawson nodded. "Good." He leaned back in his chair, balancing on its back two legs. "At least something is going right."

Again, the duke smiled. "Are you implying that having the Duke of Heathrough coming to collect his niece is not good?"

Dawson just scowled and ignored the question. He did not need Tad analyzing his feelings. "Thank you for warning me of the duke's eminent arrival." He held up the letter. "May I keep this? I should like to let Miss Petrovich read it." He smirked. "I confess I am anxious to see her reaction when she does so."

Tad nodded. "By all means, do what you wish with it." He pushed himself out of the chair, stretching his back this way and that. "Thunder and turf, Dawson. I am of a mind to procure a chair myself, to replace this abomination." He glared at the chair, as if to scare it into comfort. "But for now, I must return to Morley." He headed out the door. "I will send word when Heathrough arrives."

CHAPTER 16

Zia kneeled on the rug she had placed at the foot of Tiana's grave. It had become easier to talk with Tiana. Zia no longer felt the need to look for people who may be watching her. Speaking in Russian to her friend made her feel better and had done much to ease the nightmares.

She smoothed her skirt and fanned it out, making sure everything was hidden as it should be. Taking in a deep breath, she began. "He has returned, Tiana." She sniffed as her nose started to run. "I was so happy to see him. I know he has only been gone a week, but it felt like an eternity." Her throat tightened and she had to force a swallow so she could catch her breath. "He was as displeased with me as ever. I believe he had hoped to find me gone when he returned. And now I know not what I should do. Perhaps I should write my uncle and face whatever will come from it. Or I could just leave and tell no one where I am to go. Would moving from place to place be so bad?" But moving from this place would mean leaving Tiana behind. And Mr. Dawson and his mother. She sniffed again and wiped at her nose with the back of her hand.

She bit her lip. "My only hesitation is I do not know if I can access my inheritance. At least not in a timely manner. And by doing so, I would inform my father and thus Prince Sokolov of my whereabouts." She dropped her head into her hands for a moment. How had she believed her plans to be so clear and prudent? "Oh, Tiana. I wish you were here."

A throat cleared behind her and she jerked around, stumbling to her feet.

Mr. Dawson stood to the side of the tall gravestone in the row behind her, a large box tucked under his arm. His face was still covered in a thick mat of hair. It looked so soft, Zia nearly reached out to touch it. Did he mean to keep it for a time? She had to admit, she was inclined to agree to it staying.

Zia, suddenly self-conscious of her appearance, swatted at any snow or grass which may be clinging to her dress. "Mr. Dawson. What are you doing out in this cold weather?"

"I could ask the same of you." His voice was soft, though not angry, even if his brow held its normal creases.

Her cheeks heated. "I like to speak to Tiana." She gave a nervous laugh, twisting her hands together. "I know it sounds silly."

Mr. Dawson shook his head. "I do not think it sounds silly at all." He shifted on his feet. "Does it help? With the loneliness, I mean?" He switched his mouth to one side and looked away from her. "I mean, you have been lonely since you came here, have you not?"

Zia folded her arms across her middle, trying to keep herself from shaking in the cold. At least she believed it was the cold causing her body to tremble. "A little, I suppose. But this last week, your mother has helped to lessen those feelings."

Mr. Dawson nodded again. "I am glad for it."

Zia's eyes flicked to the box under his arm. What could be in such a large box? And where was he taking it? Was it something for the church? Why else would he come this way? There was nothing beyond the church except fields and pastures.

He noticed her gaze on the box and fumbled with it before holding it out in her direction. "I had hoped to give this to you before I left, but it was not yet finished."

She took a few steps forward and accepted the box. There was weight to whatever was inside. She kneeled back on the rug, the parcel in front of her. Slipping the ribbon from the box, she pulled off the lid to reveal a deep burgundy woolen fabric.

Zia flicked her gaze up at him, but he looked away. She pulled out the fabric and a cloak, lined with fur, unfolded in her lap. The fur looked to be similar to that from her previous cloak, but the wool was not the same.

She again looked to Mr. Dawson, her head tilted to one side.

He cleared his throat again and ran his hand along the back of his neck. "I realized that you must not be able to wear the other cloak because of the memories attached to it. I asked Mrs. Partridge, the seamstress in the village, to use the same fur but change out the wool." He finally looked at her. "I wish I could have afforded to buy a new cloak entirely, but... Well, you need to be warm if you are to spend so much time out of doors."

She pulled the cloak to her chest. The garment looked just different enough, perhaps she could wear it.

He took several steps toward her and reached down, taking the cloak from her. "Here, let me help you put it on." He held out a hand to help her to her feet.

She unfastened the cloak she had been wearing since arriving in England with shaky hands and dropped it to the ground in front of her. Her knees shook beneath her gown until Mr. Dawson draped the new cloak around her shoulders. His hand grazed her neck and she almost forgot about being cold.

"There now. Do you feel better?"

She swallowed hard and only nodded. She looked up at him. He did not look angry to see her. Would a man go to such trouble to have her cloak put to pieces if he wished her away? Perhaps he was just kind and thought only of her welfare. But perhaps, he *did* feel something more.

He took another step toward her and reached out, running his hands down her upper arms which were tucked cozily under the cloak. "You are still shivering."

"It is only from wearing no cloak for that brief moment. I will be well in a moment."

He dropped his hands and she cursed herself for her foolish words.

She closed her eyes for a moment as the warmth from the fur warmed her from the shoulders down.

A twig snapped and she opened her eyes, afraid he had left. Why could she not make a sensible decision of late? She breathed a sigh of relief to see he had only taken a small step back.

"Thank you for the cloak. Even using the same fur, this must have cost you a great deal. I will happily pay you for the expense."

His face clouded over and he shook his head. "No. There is no need. I can manage the expense."

Oh, lud. She had offended him. "I only meant to say that I know you had not planned to have me as your extended guest. I am sure my presence has cost you money you had not budgeted."

His face darkened even more.

"That is to say, I understand you wish to use as much of your funds as possible to restore Fawnbrooke. I do not wish to be the cause of any delay in those plans." Gah, why did she not stop speaking? Every word seemed only to put him in high dudgeons. "Thank you is what I meant to say. Even if I did it very poorly."

He nodded and she thought she detected a hint of a smile on

his face. Could it be true? She longed to see the slight crinkle at his eyes.

They stood there together for a moment, no one speaking, both of them vastly interested in their boots.

"There was another reason for my visit." His gaze flicked up to hers and she felt her face heat at the intensity she saw.

"Oh?"

He reached into the interior of his great coat and withdrew a folded paper. He thrust it forward.

She looked at him, her mind trying to understand what this was about. She opened the letter and her hands began to shake for another reason. This letter was from her uncle.

Zia glanced up at Mr. Dawson. "It is from my uncle." Her brow creased as she read. Her uncle said he had received a letter from her father only days before. Her father had indicated that Zia had run away, and it was believed she was coming to England. He requested that if she should contact Heathrough, that word should be sent back to Odessa immediately. The duke ended the letter by saying he would be setting out for Morley Park at once.

Zia turned the letter over in her hands, looking for any more information. When was this sent? And why was it sent to the Duke of Shearsby? She looked up at Mr. Dawson with a furrowed brow. "But how did he know where I was?"

A smile twitched at the corners of Mr. Dawson's mouth. "I would guess from the letters you sent him."

Zia licked her lips several times. Oh, yes, the letters she had been worrying over for weeks. "But I did not tell him my where-abouts. Only that I was in England." She glanced down at the frosty grass in front of her, unable to look Mr. Dawson in the eye while blatantly lying to him.

"Tad may have sent an inquiry to your uncle shortly after you woke up."

Her head jerked up and her eyes widened, her mouth dropping open. "He took a very high hand in the situation, did he not?"

Mr. Dawson's face hardened. "Did he have a choice? It seems all you have done since you awakened is tell us one fable after another. Perhaps, if you did not wish for others to intervene, *you* might have sent your uncle a letter."

Her mouth opened and closed several times. Now was her chance to confess to the lie she had told, but he looked so angry, she questioned the prudence of the idea.

"Are you implying I never sent the letter? If my uncle were here, he would call you out for the insults you have cast at my feet. I have been nothing but truthful with you, sir." She turned on her heel to return to the house, but Mr. Dawson grabbed hold of her arm and brought her back around to face him.

"Are you telling me you sent the letters to your uncle?" He stared at her, his face a stony mask.

"I do not owe you an explanation." She raised her chin high and cast him an icy stare. It was one that had sent many a servant scurrying to do her bidding, but it had little effect on the man in front of her. If anything, it only served to displease him more. He did not even seem to blink. The only indication that he was, indeed, flesh and blood was the twitching at his jawline as he grit his teeth together.

Zia shrank back. Prince Sokolov had looked on her in such a way, usually only moments before he struck her.

Mr. Dawson's hand still held her arm, but it was not tight, as Sokolov had always held her. It gave her confidence and she pulled it free with no effort at all. His face showed a fierceness that his hold did not. This man was very confusing to her.

He folded his arms across his chest. "I know you had not sent a letter before I left for Northamptonshire, madam. I heard you confess as much to this grave the day before I left."

A squeak sounded from Zia's mouth. "You...you speak Russian?"

He put his fingers in front of his face, his thumb and forefinger only a whisper apart. "*Nemnogo*—a little. Did you send the letter while I was gone?"

"But how?" She folder her arms across her stomach, all of her muscles becoming taut.

"A man who worked on our farm was from a village called Rostov, on the Don river. But that is of no import, at the moment. You did not answer my question, Princess." His mocking tone was back.

She closed her eyes. Would he strike her when she confirmed his suspicions? She shook her head. "No. I never sent the letter." She turned her head and closed an eye, bracing herself for the impact.

"What are you doing? You act as if you think I will strike you."

She straightened and looked at him. The stony expression on his face had been replaced with one of horror.

"Is that what you believed I would do?"

She bit hard on the inside of her cheek, fighting the sudden impulse to cry. "It would be your right, would it not?"

"My right? What could you possibly do which would give me the right to strike you?" He placed a hand on her arm, and she flinched.

He stepped back several paces. "You have answered my questions. I shall leave you to your conversation with your friend." He turned and stomped from the churchyard.

Zia dropped down to her knees, her head in her hands. Now that he was gone, she allowed the tears to fall. "Oh, Tiana. I did not believe I could make the situation worse, but somehow, I have. Perhaps it is best that my uncle come to fetch me at last, for Mr. Dawson shall never speak to me again. Of that I am certain."

CHAPTER 17

Dawson paced about his study, growling as often as he breathed. What an infernal girl Miss Petrovich was. She had acted so incensed with him, when she was the one who had been lying to him—imposing on his hospitality.

She had not come down from her rooms since returning from the churchyard the day before, which only seemed to make Dawson clench his fists harder. Nothing about this whole situation was working out to his benefit. Not that he had saved her in order to gain something. But should not a man at least have peace in his home after doing something noble?

He grunted and dropped heavily into his chair. He was many things, but noble was not one of them. He scratched at the hair on his face. His beard had fully taken hold by the time he returned from his trip to Somerton's estate and he had not allowed his valet to shave him clean yet. He was sure many in society would look on it with contempt, but for that he had no care.

A knock sounded at his door and Tad pushed through before Dawson could even mutter a response. The duke came in sideways, his arm tucked around a chair back. He placed the chair down in front of Dawson's desk, giving the old one a little shove to the side. Tad settled down into the new chair, a satisfied smile on his lips. "Ahhh, much better."

Dawson stared at his friend.

Tad stared back for a moment. "I told you I would not bear that chair a moment longer." He scowled at the old chair as if it were an errant child. "Now I can stay for hours, as this chair is just that comfortable."

Dawson glanced at the old chair. "Perhaps *I* prefer the old one."

Tad chuckled. "The chair was not totally the reason for my visit."

"Please, enlighten me."

Tad straightened. "The Duke of Heathrough arrived last evening. He is even now in his carriage coming here."

Dawson shot out of his seat. "He is coming here? But did you not say you would send word when he arrived?"

Tad motioned to an ivory colored paper on Dawson's desk. "I did send word. It is right there."

Dawson pulled the folded paper out from under several other letters. "Tare an' hounds. How did I not see this?" He looked up to Tad. "I assume he knows she is here?"

Tad nodded and raised a brow at Dawson. "From all your blustering, I should think such a prospect would thrill you. Have you not been wishing her gone for weeks?"

Dawson shrugged. "Yes, of course. But how do I know the man will treat her as he should?" He cleared his throat and walked around his desk, clasping his hands behind his back. "She is accustomed to being struck." Tad's brow furrowed. Dawson knew he was remembering the bruises they had discovered on Violet when first they met her. Dawson's voice quieted. "I feel a responsibility for her well-being. That is all."

Tad nodded, his face still serious for a moment. "Hmmm."

Dawson scowled at him.

"When I came in, you seemed to be scowling more than is your usual tendency. What has you in the dudgeons this morning?" Tad stood and walked toward the fireplace.

Dawson raised a shoulder and then dropped it. Had he not repeated this conversation in his own mind enough times? Did he need to put voice to his thoughts? Especially with Tad? He would no doubt find great humor in it all.

Tad pulled out his watch and clicked it open. "Well, out with it. We have little time before the duke will make his presence known."

Dawson let out another growl. "It is nothing. I confronted Miss Petrovich about her lies yesterday."

Both of Tad's brows rose to his hairline. "Oooohhhh?"

"She admitted to lying about sending the letter. She did not confess to lying about anything else, but I am inclined to think if she lies about one thing she is surely lying about the other."

Tad stood still, looking into the flames. "And this is what makes you angry? That she confessed that she did, indeed, falsify her story? I thought you already knew as much."

Dawson took in a deep breath. "I did. I just hoped I was wrong."

"You hoped she was a princess?"

Dawson shook his head. "No...oh I do not know what I hoped. The entire situation is tiresome."

"You are mad that she lied. That is it?" He ran a hand across the back of his neck. "I cannot make heads nor tails of your reasoning these days." His brow creased. "I find I am a little concerned. I have never seen you in such a state."

Dawson folded his arms across his chest. "She had the audacity to be angry with me for catching her in her lies. Me. After I have shown her such hospitality and kindness."

Tad guffawed. "You? Hospitable and kind? I am sorry to have missed such a display."

One eye squinted at Tad as Dawson pursed his lips shut. Was Tad merely jesting, or did he truly not think Dawson capable of kindness? Dawson was often grumpy and churlish, but that did not mean he held no kindness within him, did it?

Tad put a hand on Dawson's back. "I am only jesting, my friend. I, more than anyone, know of your generous nature."

A knock sounded and Mrs. Hardy slipped inside the room at Dawson's approval. "Sir, the Duke of Heathrough has come. He says he is here to collect his niece." She raised a knowing brow. "Shall I send for the girl?"

Dawson nodded. "Yes, please ask Miss Petrovich to join us."

Mrs. Hardy gave a nod. "He is in the morning room, sir. I shall have tea sent in immediately."

Dawson was grateful for this woman. Indeed, he had been most fortunate in all of his staff. Granted, most of them had come from the staff at Morley Park, so it seemed Tad was again whom he should be grateful to.

Tad squeezed Dawson's shoulder. "Are you ready for this? You are about to receive the answers to questions you have had for nearly a month."

Dawson sucked in a breath, his stomach twisting, his earlier meal feeling uneasy in his belly. "Now I find I do not wish to know the answers."

Tad's head nodded slightly. "I know, my friend. I know."

They moved down the corridor and stood in front of the morning room door. Dawson's arms felt heavy and weak. Perhaps if neither he, nor Miss Petrovich ever entered the room, they could just continue on the way they had for the last month. Suddenly, that seemed a perfectly acceptable solution.

He rotated his shoulders. He was acting like a boy in calf-love. Squaring himself to the door, he pushed it open, Tad following behind him.

A short, rather rotund man, much beyond his prime, stood before the fireplace with his hands outstretched. He turned when Dawson and Tad entered and clasped his hands behind his back. Looking at Heathrough head on, Dawson could see why the man was known for his unyielding opinions. While he was older, his eyes were clear and sharp and his demeanor stoic.

Tad stepped between the two men. "His Grace, the Duke of Heathrough, it is my honor to introduce you to Mr. Dugray Dawson of Fawnbrooke." Both men sketched shallow bows, neither one breaking eye contact with the other.

Heathrough rose and shifted his gaze, looking at the room. "I do not believe Fawnbrooke is anything to recommend Mr. Dawson."

Tad slapped Dawson on the back. "It will be, I can assure you. Once Dawson has had a chance to make the needed repairs."

Dawson clasped his hands behind his back, annoyed that the duke would insult him in his own home, no less.

"The estate aside," Tad continued, "Mr. Dawson here is the man who found the carriage after the accident and rescued the survivor."

The old duke's stony appearance did not falter. "I thank you for the kindness, sir. I hope you have not sullied my niece's reputation any."

Dawson could stone face with the best of them. He knew he should feel intimidated by the duke, but he did not. Perhaps that would be to his detriment. "My mother has been in residence for the entirety of your niece's stay. She has acted as an attentive chaperone. I can assure you, your niece's reputation is still intact." If she was indeed his niece. *Oh, please don't let her be his niece.* He could dismiss the lies, could he not? His mother was correct. They all had secrets they had kept.

The door creaked open and Zia walked into the room. Why had he never recognized how gracefully she walked? Her head was held high and she nearly floated across the floor. He knew then—indeed, he had known for some time that she was as she claimed. His shoulders dropped a fraction. She was the princess.

She looked up at him, waiting for an introduction. Dawson was speechless. His time with her was coming to a close. She was the duke's niece. He would surely take her with him when he left here, in only moments, judging by the way the duke looked about the room with a turned-up nose. It was the same look Zia had given the room her first day here. In point of fact, the duke's nose looked very similar to Zia's.

Dawson's chest tightened. Every new thing he noticed only seemed to be taking her away from Fawnbrooke. He commanded his mind to quit its assessment of everyone and everything. If he did not make the connections, could he manage to keep her here?

Tad stepped in when Dawson seemed uninclined to make the proper introductions. "Your Grace. This is the woman I wrote you about. She claims to be your niece, but we had nothing, save her word, to confirm such details. We had hoped you had something which could give the confirmation we need.

The duke looked her up and down and Dawson felt his hands clench. If any other man had looked at Zia in such a way, he would have called him out. He loosened his grip. It was only what one would do for a person he was responsible for.

Dawson breathed a sigh. Who was telling a bouncer now? He did not want her to go not because he was responsible for her, but because he loved her.

The duke took Zia by the arms and turned her to the side, staring at her profile. "I have a miniature of my sister's family. She sent it to me several years ago. This girl looks older than the girl in the picture, but that is to be expected." He gave firm nod. "I find I am not in need of the picture. This is my niece. She looks very much like her mother." The duke's mask broke only for a moment as sadness entered his eyes. He awkwardly reached for Zia's hands. "It is a pleasure to finally make your acquaintance, my dear."

A painful breath squeezed through Dawson's clenched teeth and his throat ached. He had fallen in love with a princess. He was a dolt. He had known there was a possibility, and yet he had allowed it to happen anyway. Even though there was no chance for a match.

Zia curtsied. "And you, Uncle. Thank you for coming to fetch me. I am sorry to have caused you any inconvenience." She flicked her gaze to Dawson.

He expected to see a superior look in her eye, one that said she had been telling the truth, all along. But all he saw was fear, hesitation, and sadness. Could she be feeling as apprehensive about her leaving as he was?

The duke released her hands and gave her a little pat on the arm. "Shearsby has agreed to have you stay with me at Morley Park for a few days' time, after which you will return with me to Chatney House."

Zia swallowed. "And what then, Uncle? Shall you send me back to Odessa?"

"This is not the time or the place to discuss such things, child." Dawson was relieved to see the duke's features soften. "Go have a maid pack your trunk. We shall leave as soon as you are ready."

Could it be the duke was not the fiend Dawson feared him to be, even if Dawson desired it? Still he did not fully trust him. The duke did not know Zia as Dawson did. Would he do what was best for her? His mouth felt dry and the room felt colder. Dawson rubbed his hand over his beard. He felt Zia watching him.

She flicked her gaze away from him and back to her uncle. "I have no trunks. They were destroyed in the accident. Indeed, I have very little. I can pack all of it in a valise."

The duke nodded. "Yes, I forgot about the accident for a moment. You lost your maid as well, yes?"

Tears formed in Zia's eyes. She did well to push them back, but still it tugged at Dawson's heart. He had not considered the fact that Zia leaving Fawnbrooke also meant leaving Tiana, *her maid.*

The duke cleared his throat, obviously uncomfortable with his niece and her emotions. "No need to become a watering pot, now. You may say your goodbyes to your maid before we quit the county. But for now, I wish to return to Morley Park. Hurry along now, child."

Zia bit her lower lip but turned and walked toward the door. Her steps looked heavy and slow.

Dawson needed to do something, but what he was not sure. Embrace her? Speak with her? He knew not what the best course of action was in this situation. He only knew he felt helpless to make her feel better. And that made him feel as though someone had reached inside him and pulled out his heart.

CHAPTER 18

Zia held the books in her hands, clutching them to her chest. She wanted to keep them, keep something of his close by her. But she knew how much these books meant to Mr. Dawson.

She knocked softly on the door to his study. No one answered. She looked down the corridor both directions but found no one in sight. Turning the handle, she pushed the door open. The room was even more warm and inviting than the last time she was in here. Perhaps it felt so because she knew him better.

Zia walked on tiptoes to his desk, a feeling of reverence filling the room. She dropped down to flat feet. That was just silly. This was not a church or cemetery. It was simply Mr. Dawson's study. She set the books down, trailing her finger over the wooden desktop.

"I thought you would be in you chambers packing."

Zia jumped and turned toward the doorway.

Mr. Dawson stood, his arms folded across his chest, leaning against the frame.

"Begging you pardon, Mr. Dawson." Zia grabbed the books from off the desk and held them up. "I only thought to return your books before I left for Morley Park with my uncle."

He stood up straight and walked toward her. "Thank you." His hand brushed hers as he grasped the books. She reluctantly let him take them from her hand.

She stared at him. "The others are in my chambers. I shall have Lucy return them to you."

He set the books back down on the desk and took another step toward her. A book would scarcely fit between them, so close they were to each other. He took in a deep breath. "I am sure you'll find Morley much more to your standards and liking."

Zia shook her head, her fingertips tracing the grain of the wood on the desk. "I do not know how that could be true. I have come to love Fawnbrooke. I shall be most disheartened to leave it, and you..." She tilted her head to the side. "That is to say, your mother. I shall miss her very much as well."

"You are always welcome here, should you ever come back to Leicestershire." He glanced down at the rug at his feet. "I must also beg your forgiveness. I have been unforgivably rude to you, calling you princess even when I thought you could not possibly be one. I should have believed you from the beginning."

Zia reached out a hand, placing it on his forearm. He flinched at her touch and looked up at her. "Had I seen me in the inn, as you did, I probably should not have believed me either." She chuckled. "It was just as I had planned. Only I did not realize my plan was so wholly convincing. I rather had thought Tiana had bungled the part of a lady."

Dawson lifted a hand but dropped it back to his side. "Had I not been so decidedly against the notion of you being a princess, I should have seen it sooner. You do not carry yourself as a maid would." His brow puckered and Zia thought he would back up.

But he didn't. "And now you are for Morley Park and from thence to Derbyshire."

"I do not wish to go. I want to stay here at Fawnbrooke—with your mother." She reached up and touched his beard. It was just as soft as she had imagined. When had she become so brazen?

His eyes closed for a moment, but when he opened them, there was determination there. Just what he was determined to do, she did not know. He gently took her hand from his face, holding it in his own. He traced the length of her fingers. "Your presence will be missed." He released her hand, allowing it to drop away. "My mother has grown quite fond of you."

Ask me to stay. She willed him to do her bidding, knowing if he did, she would never leave him. Surely, he felt something for her. Is that not what she saw in his gaze?

He took another step back. "Heathrough is waiting, Princess."

With that he turned and walked quickly from the room. Zia turned her back to the door, lest he come back in and see her tears. He did not want her. Her dreams had only been that of a childish girl.

Zia kept to her chambers after arriving at Morley Park, choosing to take a tray in her room rather than go below and eat with the others. The Duchess of Shearsby had been kind and understanding, as she always was, but Zia wanted to be alone. She sighed. Perhaps *wanted* was not the right word, because indeed, she did not want to be alone. She wanted to be at Fawnbrooke with Mrs. Dawson. She would not allow other desires into her mind.

Loneliness was not foreign to her. She had felt it for years. Only recently had it been pushed aside. But now she was to be forced to stay here at Morley Park and then on to Chatney House.

Beyond that, she knew not. All were places full of strangers and people she felt wholly unconnected to. It seemed she was destined to be alone. But in truth, if Mr. Dawson did not want her, did she care where she ended up? A dull thumping started behind her eyes, moving up her forehead and along the top of her head.

She moved to the chair by the window and picked up the pieces of sewing she had brought with her. Her uncle had insisted they could purchase her a new wardrobe, but Zia had wanted to bring her unfinished dress with her anyway. She would try to finish it on her own, even if Mrs. Dawson would never know if she did so or not. Although, Zia doubted she had the knowledge to complete such a task without the older woman's guidance.

She placed the fabric in her lap. Perhaps the monotony of the stitches would help take her mind off Mr. Dawson and Mother D, and everything about Fawnbrooke. But after several misplaced stitches, she gave up the effort. The only thing she truly enjoyed about sewing was doing it with Mother D and the conversation they enjoyed while doing it. This—she threw it into the basket at her side—this sewing was tiresome and dull. Perhaps she would never finish the dress. What did she care? She picked up the fabric again and ran her hand over the soft, smooth surface. The kind face of Mother D hovered in her mind.

Zia took in a deep breath. She *would* finish the dress, but perhaps not until her emotions had calmed, and a headache was not threatening. She folded the fabric neatly and placed it inside the basket, placing it on the floor beside the dressing table. Going to the bedside table, she chose a book from the stack. *Emma*. This was the copy Mr. Dawson had purchased early in her stay at Fawnbrooke. The whole stack had been purchased by him. Though she had told him she would have Lucy return them to his study, when packing her things, she found she could not leave the books behind. Instead, she had left a note and money on the side table in her room. He could use the money and buy whatever books he wished to have for his library, as she doubted very much he had wanted gothic novels and books on romance filling his library shelves in the first place.

She sat back in the chair and opened the book to the place marked with a silken ribbon. She had already read the story twice, but it was no matter. She enjoyed the antics of Miss Woodhouse. In truth, she enjoyed this much more than even the gothic novels, although they were enjoyable in a different way.

Not more than a dozen words into the page, her mind began to wander. Why could she not be allowed a moment's peace? Why could she not cast his image from her memory?

Her uncle had been cordial, and she conceded that her fears of him had been without merit. But still he had not indicated what he planned to do with her beyond taking her back to Chatney House.

Zia closed the book, her finger inserted to mark the page, and looked outside the window. She missed the window seat in the North Parlor at Fawnbrooke. It had a lovely view and a most comfortable cushion. Not that the view from her room at Morley was not acceptable. It was, indeed, more than lovely. All of Morley was lovely. It reminded her of her home in Odessa—grand and imposing. Perhaps that was why she did not care for it so much.

She would never have thought it possible to prefer the more modest and comfortable surroundings of Fawnbrooke. But her current doldrums seemed to indicate that perhaps she did. She knew it was more than the estate she preferred. She preferred *him,* above any other gentleman of her acquaintance. Indeed, she loved him. But he had cast her aside.

She traced her finger on the window as a form came into view. While it was far away, Zia knew immediately it was Mr. Dawson. Even if the beard had not given him away, his broad shoulders and the confident way he walked would have. Mr. Dawson walked with a sort of hitch in his step. Zia had never really thought much of it until now. She could not say as to when she had begun to take such notice of him. Now she wondered if there was an injury that had caused the hitch or if it was simply the way of him. He entered Morley Park's stables, taking him from her view.

Zia pushed herself out of the chair once more, dropping her book onto the cushion. She paced in front of the window, her gaze bouncing from the stables below to the wardrobe and back. She wrung her hands in front of her and bit at her lower lip. Could she grab her cloak and make it to the stable before he left? What would she say to him if she did see him? It would seem quite untoward of her to seek him out, without some other reason for her to be in the stable. But what business did she have in the stable? Her mind worked. She had no horse here at Morley, so it seemed unlikely she should need to check on one.

She made another pass in front of the window. She did enjoy horses. Could that not be enough of an excuse? She shook her head, her breath coming out in short, huffy spurts. The stable doors opened and the duke and Mr. Dawson both stepped out into the cold. Mr. Dawson pulled his coat tighter around him. Would the duke invite him inside for tea? Zia glanced down at her dress, wishing she had her trunks with her.

He turned enough that she could vaguely see his face. His beard hid most of it, but the slight crinkle and squint of his eyes told her that he was smiling. Her heart squeezed. She had not seen him smile in days. Obviously, he was not as distressed by her removal from Fawnbrooke as she was.

Zia sat down in the chair, still watching him from her window. She picked her book back up, forcing herself to pull her gaze from him. While she may wish to see him—speak to him— it did not appear the same held true for Mr. Dawson. Why was she continuing to torture herself? The memories of him were bad enough, must she subject herself to the real thing?

But even as she thought it, her eyes drifted to the stable doors. Mr. Dawson and the duke were not to be seen. She glanced at her door. Was he even now within the house? How was it she could feel both desire and despair at the thought of seeing him? She gave her head a hard shake as she mentally scolded herself, trying to refocus on her novel. When had she become such a silly girl, unable to make up her mind or control her emotions? Her mother had taught her better than this.

A knock sounded and Zia started at the sound. The maid assigned to her at her arrival entered the room. Zia had not even asked the girl her name, knowing she would not be here long enough for it to matter. She dipped a curtsy, her eyes never rising above the hem of Zia's gown. "Her Grace was hoping you might join her for tea, Your Highness."

Zia wished to decline, wished to stay in her chambers and read or sew, anything but talk to people and be forced to act as if everything was well and good when it was not. Indeed, it was quite the opposite. She was hurt and confused. But she knew it would be rude to decline the invitation from the duchess, so she nodded. "Tell Her Grace I should be delighted to join her."

The maid nodded. "I shall deliver the message. Do you wish me to return and help you change into half dress?"

Zia shook her head. "I would not think it necessary even if I had such a dress, which I do not." Zia frowned. She had never thought the duchess overly formal, but Zia did not really know her all that well. "If it will offend Her Grace for me to still be in my morning dress, then perhaps it would be best if I declined."

The maid shook her head. "Oh, no. I cannot imagine Her Grace will mind in the least. She is a most kind mistress. I only thought that because you are a—that is to say, I believed it was what you would want." She dipped a curtsy. "Begging your pardon, Your Highness. I shall inform Her Grace that you will be down shortly."

Zia smiled. The girl was all fluttering and apologies since Zia had arrived. One would think serving a duke and duchess would give the girl some degree of confidence. Although, from what Zia had seen of the duke and duchess, they were not typical of their class.

"You need not apologize."

The girl curtsied again. "Yes, I am sorry." She caught herself. "That is to say, very good, Princess." Then slipped from the room.

Zia waited in the corridor while the maid announced her presence to the duchess. She heard a muffled acceptance and the maid opened the door for Zia to enter.

The duchess was sitting on a pale green brocade sofa situated near the fire. She looked up at Zia's entrance and stood, coming toward her with hands extended. "Ah, Your Highness. Thank you for joining me. Please do come sit down."

Zia returned the smile but found it difficult to mean it. A wave of guilt flooded over her. From all accounts, even those few interactions Zia had already had, the duchess was a perfectly amiable woman. And yet, Zia felt incapable of reciprocating such feelings. But she had been taught protocols and knew how to falsely display pleasure.

The duchess motioned to a blonde woman standing in front of the opposite sofa. "This is my sister, Lady Munsford."

The woman dipped a shallow curtsy.

The duchess led Zia over to the couch. She sat down and poured out the tea, handing a cup to Zia and to Lady Munsford.

"I hope you have found your chambers to your satisfaction." The duchess seemed more uncertain than she had last Zia had been here. Did the knowledge of her title make them believe she was a different person now? Zia actually missed being treated as a falsifier.

"I am sure they are nothing compared to what you are used to, but I do hope they are adequate." The duchess ran her thumb back and forth along the rim of the saucer in her hands.

Zia tilted her head to the side. "Indeed, your home reminds me very much of the estate where I grew up in Odessa."

The duchess seemed to relax a fraction at the admission. Had she truly thought Zia would find Morley lacking? Zia looked around the room. How could someone ever think this house lacking in any way?

Lady Munsford seemed content to keep her thoughts to herself, watching her sister and Zia instead.

The duchess took a sip of her tea as silence descended upon the room.

Zia set her cup on the tray and took a small sandwich. This whole interaction only seemed to validate Zia's earlier conclusions. She was meant to be alone.

The door from the corridor opened and Zia's gaze shot to it. Perhaps Mr. Dawson had been invited to join them for tea. Her pulse quickened and her body heated. But her gaze dropped to her hands when the duke entered alone.

He moved to the settee opposite Zia and placed a kiss on his wife's cheek before lowering himself onto the cushion next to her. They sat very close to each other and Zia found it difficult to watch. She'd had similar dreams of a life with Mr. Dawson.

The duchess poured her husband a cup, but from a second pot.

Zia's brow furrowed. Did he think himself so above them that he could not even have tea from the same pot? This notion did not ring true based on her other interactions with the duke.

Lady Munsford finally spoke. "Do not mind Shearsby. He prefers chocolate to tea." She cast a glance at her sister. "I am sure there is plenty if it be your preference also."

The duchess colored slightly.

Zia leaned forward, her mouth turned down in distaste. "I can assure you I am quite happy with the tea."

The duchess perplexed Zia. She was refined and moved with the grace of a queen, yet at times she seemed uncertain of herself. Not the typical actions of a duchess at all.

"When I was younger, we had an envoy from Spain come to visit the Russian royal court. He spent several nights at our estate in Odessa before he continued on to St. Petersburg. They brought the chocolate drink with them and presented some to my father. I admit, I found it most distasteful."

The duchess laughed. "I find it tolerable, but I confess I prefer tea as well."

The duke shrugged. "It only means there is more for me." He raised his cup as if toasting them and took a drink. He seemed to be the only person not intimidated by her title.

Zia found herself hard pressed not to smile for real. The duke had a certain way about him, but she could not put her finger on what exactly it was. Something about him made her want to relax and open up to him. Or at the very least, let her guard down.

He stared at her over his cup, his eyes assessing her. "I have invited Mr. Dawson and his mother to join us for supper this evening."

Zia's pulse jumped again, and she saw the duke's eyes drop to her neck. She absently placed her fingers to the spot where her pulse throbbed. Could the duke actually see it? Did he know what his announcement had done to her? She cleared her throat. "I will be happy to see Mrs. Dawson again."

The duke's brows rose slightly. "*Mrs.* Dawson, you say?"

Zia nodded, not trusting her voice.

The duke took another sip of his chocolate, his gaze never leaving her. "Yes, I find I quite enjoy her company."

The duchess patted him on the leg. "There now, Tad. I believe you have studied our guest long enough." She cast an apologetic look at Zia. "Perhaps you have some business in your study which needs your attention?"

He looked down at his wife. "I believe you wish to be rid of me, my dear." His mouth turned down.

She smiled up at him. "You are partially correct." The duchess flicked her gaze to Zia. "I believe our guest wishes you away. I am only seeing to her comfort." She flicked her hands in front of her. "Now shoo." The duchess placed several sandwiches and even more cakes onto a plate and handed it to her husband. "There now. I shall not deprive you of sustenance. You may continue your assessment of Her Highness this evening."

Zia knew the duchess's words were intended to put Zia more at ease, but the thought that the duke would resume his penetrating looks this evening only proved to keep her on edge.

CHAPTER 19

Dawson straightened his waistcoat for what must have been the hundredth time. He checked his hair and his freshly shaven face in the mirror hanging in the entryway at Morley.

"You look very handsome, Dugray. You need not fuss so much."

"I am not fussing, Mother." Dawson looked past his mother, unable to look directly at her and lie. "My face is merely chilled after the removal of my beard."

His mother smiled. "I think it worth it to see your handsome face."

He growled low in his throat. He had never felt this nervous when dinning with Tad and Violet in the past. Indeed, Dawson had dined with them for over two years. Not every night, but enough to make his current fidgeting odd and disconcerting. While it would be easier to have Miss Petrovich, or rather, Her Highness—

He shook his head in frustration. Zia. Yes, that was better.

While it would be better to have Zia away from Leicestershire for good, he dreaded the thought of never seeing her again. No doubt, spending the evening in the same room would be difficult, but he was grateful to have one last night with her.

"Mr. Dawson. Mrs. Dawson. If you will please follow me to the drawing room."

Dawson held out his arm to his mother and escorted her down the corridor. They were almost to the door. He would see Zia any moment and his pulse could stop its incessant thrumming.

The door opened, but Zia was not within. The room was completely empty. Dawson's whole body sagged-not only in relief, but also disappointment.

Dawson led his mother to the settee and helped her sit, but he did not join her on the couch. Instead, he paced the distance in front of the fireplace.

The door swung open and Baker stepped inside. "Her Highness, Princess Zia Petrovich," the butler said.

Zia stood in the doorway and it was as if an entire swarm of bee's converged in Dawson's stomach. Had it only been a day since last he saw her? It felt like months.

She walked toward the couch and Dawson paused in his pacing. He was unable to take his eyes off her. She was not wearing an evening gown; he had seen this same dress several times during her stay at Fawnbrooke. Nor was her hair done in a particularly intricate way. And yet, she was as lovely, if not more so, than he had ever seen her.

Since her uncle had arrived and taken her away, Dawson had been telling himself that it was all for the best. She could never be happy with him and he knew he could not be happy if she was not. But seeing her here, standing in front of him, he knew he would not be happy without her, either. He was, as he had always believed, destined to be unhappy and alone.

He swallowed hard and bowed. "Princess." The word came out strangled. All the times he had called her by her title flooded into his mind. It had started as a jab, to show his disdain for her and her lies. But at some point, it had changed. Dawson could not say just when it had happened. He no longer felt disdain, nor anything resembling it. When he used her title now, it was with the utmost respect. "It is a pleasure to see you again. I hope your stay at Morley has suited you."

Zia nodded. "The duke and duchess have been more than accommodating." She leaned forward and embraced Dawson's mother. "Good evening, Mother D." Her brow furrowed. "I suppose I should not call you such anymore."

His mother shook her head. "Nonsense, dear."

Dawson's stomach gurgled and burned as the acid churned inside him. He was a nodcock to be jealous of his own mother.

"I have missed your company since you departed Fawnbrooke." His mother patted her hand.

"I find I feel precisely the same way. Her Grace is very friendly, but our conversations pale in comparison to those you and I shared."

As if on cue, Tad and Violet came into the room. "Ah, Dawson, you are come." The duke clasped him on the shoulder and squeezed. He then turned to Dawson's mother and leaned in, placing a quick kiss on her cheek. "I am glad you are joining us as well, Mother D." He lifted his shoulders, his head shaking slightly. "I find I still cannot get over the notion that you are here in England." He waved the thought away. "I am certain it will pass in time."

The group moved toward the couches, still waiting for Heathrough and Lord and Lady Munsford.

Dawson had wished to hold his arm out for Zia to take, but he held back so as not to leave his mother unaccompanied. Besides, he was not a social equal to a princess, no matter how he had begun to think of her over the past month.

The ladies and Tad found seats on the fainting couch and several chairs near the fireplace, while Dawson stood to the side, staring out the window into the darkness.

He should have declined the invitation when Tad had asked him to supper this afternoon. What was he thinking? He let out a breath and rubbed his hand across the back of his neck. He had wanted to see Zia again, but he had not anticipated it being this painful. It was not unlike giving a small crust of bread to a starving man. It was not enough to stave off the hunger, only enough to make him wish for more.

The door opened and the Duke of Heathrough and Lord and Lady Munsford stepped into the room together. Baker announced them and then announced supper.

Dawson walked to the cluster of chairs and helped his mother stand. He bit his cheek and offered a hand to Zia. He was being presumptuous, he knew, but this was his last chance with her. To his ridiculous relief she accepted it and he helped her to her feet. Perhaps he need not feel so apprehensive around her. He let a smile come to his lips.

He held his arm out to his mother and Zia, but Heathrough cleared his throat and Zia placed her arm on her uncle's.

His smile fell away. How could he have thought his attentions would be welcome?

She cast a look over her shoulder at Dawson. He thought he saw regret, but he could not be sure. He was unsure of so much of late.

He shook his head. Life would be better when she has quit the county entirely.

Dawson ate in relative silence, the low hum of the voices around him barely discernable past the thoughts swirling in his head. How different his life was from only a few months before. He was landowner, a master of an estate. His mother was here. And Zia--he flicked his gaze across the table.

It was not the first time Dawson's gaze wandered over to Zia, but she seemed more interested in her plate than in looking at him. It was just as well.

His mouth was pulled down in a frown and he found himself at a loss to do anything about it.

"Do you not agree, Dawson?"

He pushed his food around his plate.

"Dawson?"

Tad nearly yelled his name, and Dawson flinched, looking up. "Begging your pardon?" He looked around the table at the smiling faces of everyone seated there. Everyone but Zia. She seemed as preoccupied as he.

"I was telling Heathrough about our good fortune in purchasing horses on our recent trip."

Dawson glanced at Tad and then at Heathrough and nodded. "Yes. It was a successful trip. I should think by spring next, we should have several foals."

Heathrough nodded, his raised brows indicating he was moderately impressed. "I understand you have purchased the offspring of *Eclipse*. That is a coup, indeed. I do not know how you convinced the old earl to sell to you. I have it on good authority that many before you have tried unsuccessfully."

Dawson looked to Tad. "I have friends who helped make it possible." Dawson had wondered why the earl chose to sell to him. He knew Tad easily made friends, but the Earl of Somerton was not known for his congeniality. Though, Dawson *had* paid more for the foal than the earl had told them at the onset. Dawson had been ready to walk away, but Tad had taken the earl aside and when they returned, the price was higher than the original, but

160

lower than what the earl had asked for only a few moments earlier. Tad would not tell Dawson what he had told the earl and Dawson had not pressed him for the information. But it had likely come at a high price to his friend.

Heathrough turned his attentions to Tad. "I assume you helped play a part."

Tad shrugged. "Only a minor roll." He glanced at Dawson. "Dugray is the best horseman I've ever known. I merely made the earl see the wisdom of selling the foal to someone as capable as my friend."

Dawson normally cringed when people, other than his mother, called him by his Christian name. But in this instance, the compliment overshadowed any irritation he might have felt. Tad had said as much to Dawson many times, but to hear him say such things to Heathrough meant more than words could say.

Heathrough nodded. "I should like to come and see for myself next year." He shrugged. "I am a fair judge of horseflesh myself."

Dawson dipped his head. "I should be honored to show you. It will take a few years yet, but I believe we shall have a success of it." He always included Tad when speaking of the business. Even though it was Dawson running it and funding the majority of it, Tad had already put up money against the first foal born.

"Yes, I should think you will eventually. If that estate of yours does not drive you to financial ruin first."

Dawson bristled. "I contend that the estate will rival any in England, or Scotland for that matter, once I am through with it." He sat back in his seat and picked up his fork by the tines, dropping it lightly back to the table. "Fawnbrooke has great potential."

The old duke shrugged. "Many have tried before you and failed. Why should you be any different?"

Lord Munsford set down his fork. "I, for one, am hoping you

do make a go of it. I like to see people prove society wrong." He looked at Rose and she smiled at him. "It's a notion I live by."

Dawson leaned forward with both elbows on the table. "None that failed before *were me*, Your Grace. Therein lies the difference. I do not go into endeavors such as these without a solid plan. Fawnbrooke will be successful." He sat back in his seat, hoping that Heathrough did not detect the quiver of doubt he felt. No matter how hard he tried, he still struggled to fight the part of him that suspected there may be more of his father in him than he wished to admit.

"I agree with Mr. Dawson. I have seen his tenacity. If anyone can make Fawnbrooke successful, it is he."

Dawson glanced from the duke to Zia. For the first time, she stared back at him, a soft smile curving her lips. Zia believed in him? His chest warmed.

Heathrough grunted. "I wish you luck then, Mr. Dawson." He looked from Dawson to his niece and then back again. His brow furrowed. "I will be happy to be proven wrong, in this case."

Dawson looked at the duke and gave him a firm nod. "You shall be greatly surprised when you come and view the new foals next spring. And not just by the horses. There will be marked improvement in the estate as well. I can assure you of such." Why was he still talking? Boasting that there would be marked changes after only a year? That was not much time to make a go of Fawnbrooke.

Dawson pinched his lips shut tight, just in case he felt inclined to make other grand predictions about his estate or any other aspects of his life.

The men declined after supper drinks, in favor of joining the woman in the drawing room. Dawson and Tad rarely held to the tradition, except when company was present. Neither man smoked pipes or cigars as was quickly becoming popular and they were not much for drinking strong liquor either. When Heathrough and Munsford did not insist upon the separation, they all adjourned into the drawing room together.

Dawson and Lord Munsford sat in chairs opposite the fireplace. Tad, Violet and his mother occupied one couch, while Zia, Heathrough and Rose sat on the other. It gave Dawson a good vantage point to see everyone in the group, but he found himself only looking at one person. That is, until she would look in his direction and then he found it necessary to look at anything but her.

Dawson's leg bounced up and down. He pushed himself out of his chair, taking his restlessness to a clear path in front of the windows. Why did Heathrough have to linger on here any longer? He had what he came for, why could not leave and allow Dawson to begin the process of forgetting about Zia?

Heathrough wandered over to him. "I see the way you look at my niece, sir."

Dawson pulled up short. "And how is that, Your Grace?" He clasped his hands behind his back. What was he to stay to such a remark?

"You love her, that much is obvious. And you must want what is best for her, which is why you are not pursuing a match." Dawson frowned. He should not be surprised by Heathrough's observations. The man was known to have a keen mind. But what of Zia? Had she seen it also? Could she ever feel the same?

He cleared his throat. "I'm sure you realize the difference in your stations is too great. She could never lower herself to marry you."

Dawson felt his throat tighten. He knew these facts, had told himself this exact thing dozens of times. Yet it hurt to have someone else tell him he was not good enough. "I will make a success of Fawnbrooke."

The duke nodded. "Yes, I am certain you will, but it will make no difference. Even if you were one of the richest men in England, you have no title. You hail from no nobility. She is the great-grand-daughter of a Tzar. I could not in good conscience condone such an association."

"Thank you for your warning. But as you surmised, I had no intention of asking the princess for her hand in marriage. Now, if you will excuse me." He moved to the globe on the stand in the corner, needing some separation. He found England and traced his finger across the channel and onto the continent, until he found Odessa. He sighed. If she returned to Russia, they would quite literally be a world apart.

The door to the drawing room opened and Baker entered. He approached Heathrough and bowed, handing him a folded paper. "This just came for you, Your Grace. It was forwarded on from Chatney House."

Heathrough took the paper and dismissed the butler. He looked at the paper, seemingly uncertain whether to crack the seal or to put the paper into his pocket to read later. He turned the letter over and ran a finger over the seal.

Zia snatched the letter from Heathrough's hands. "That is my father's seal." She looked at her uncle with wide eyes. She clearly wanted to open it, but Dawson knew she was not comfortable enough with the man to demand such things.

Heathrough nodded. "Yes, I believe it is." He frowned at it and then pushed himself up. "Let *me* discover what it says." He snatched it back again.

Tad moved to the edge of his seat. "Would you like us to leave you while you read it?"

The duke shook his head. "No need. I do not need complete privacy." He walked to the other side of the room and cracked the seal. The room fell completely silent, everyone looking from Zia to Heathrough and back.

Zia looked as if she might launch herself at her uncle and grab the letter for herself, or else loose the meager amount of dinner she had managed to eat.

Dawson moved over and sat on the couch next to her. He wanted to take her hand and hold it, offer some sort of comfort, but he did not feel it his right to do so. He did receive a hint of satisfaction when she scooted back into the couch and thus closer to him. Had she intentionally moved closer to him? He felt as if she had, but most likely he was imagining only what he *wished* to be true.

After what felt an eternity, the duke returned to the cluster of seats where they all sat waiting. He looked at Dawson, as if he wished his seat back, but Dawson ignored him. He wanted to be close to Zia when she learned what was in the letter. She was nervous, he could tell. Even more than that, she was scared.

Seeing that Dawson was not about to abandon his post, Heathrough sat in the chair Dawson had previously occupied. "It is, indeed, from your father." Heathrough took in a breath. "He is in England and on his way to Chatney House. I dare say he may be arriving as we speak."

Zia chewed on her bottom lip. "Did he make any mention of Prince Sokolov?"

Her uncle nodded. "It seems they are together, come to take you back to Odessa, my dear."

Zia sucked in a breath and her face blanched. "Prince Sokolov has come too." She closed her eyes and dropped her head into her hands.

CHAPTER 20

"What am I to do? I will not go back with him. After all I have done..." Her father would be unhappy with her, but he would likely forgive her once he knew she was safe, and after she had apologized.

But Sokolov? He would most certainly kill her when they were alone at last. Zia was almost certain of it. Sokolov was not a man to brook such behavior from a female, nor allow his reputation to be sullied in such a way. If he decided to spare her life, it would only be so he could torture her over and over again.

She sat up straight, looking around the room for a means of escape. She could not stay here any longer. Two days—if she even had that much time—was not enough space between them. Her stomach roiled again, and she thought this time she might actually be sick.

A strong hand rested on her arm. "You cannot run forever." Mr. Dawson's voice was soft and comforting.

"What choice do I have?" She moved to the edge of the couch, perched for flight.

"I will not let him take you, not unless you wish to go." Mr. Dawson held her gaze. "But if you run, he will find you again. And then you will have no one to protect you."

She shook her head. "You do not know Sokolov. He will not give you the option. He takes what he wants, and nothing will stand in his way. I was foolish to think I could escape him."

"He cannot be as bad as all that, can he?" Heathrough looked questioningly at her, as if he did not believe her story. Why did no one believe what she said? Did she not have an honest face?

Mr. Dawson glowered at the duke. "I am certain he is every bit the scoundrel the princess asserts."

Mr. Dawson believed her? After all the lies she had told him? He was one to believe her now? It seemed impossible. And yet, he looked on her with very concerned eyes.

"Sokolov is not afraid to rule with his fist, if need be. There is a very dark side to him." She looked at her hands, suddenly afraid to make eye contact with anyone in the room, as if speaking of Sokolov alone was enough to make her cower. "A side I have encountered on more than one occasion."

Shock registered on Heathrough's face and he sat forward in his chair. "But surely, once your father knows of your wishes, he will not make you marry the man. He must have learned of Sokolov's true character?"

Zia looked up, meeting her uncle's gaze. "That was my belief at first. But Sokolov only shows his best when my father is in his presence. My father chose to believe Sokolov's lies rather than his own daughter. Even when I had bruises to prove the truthfulness of my claims. Sokolov had stories to explain everything away."

Her uncle's brow crinkled. "I shall offer you my protection."

Zia wrung her hands. "As I told Mr. Dawson, that will not be enough."

A thought struck her, but she dismissed it. It would not be fair to Mr. Dawson.

Shearsby leaned over with his elbows on his knees. "You do not believe the power of two dukes would be enough to protect you?"

Zia lifted her shoulders. "Perhaps in the eyes of the law. But Sokolov will wait until I am alone. And then he will take what is his...or what he believes is his. Once out of England, your laws will have no hold."

Mrs. Dawson looked stricken. "Then what are we to do? How are we to protect you?"

Did she dare put forth her idea? She glanced at Mr. Dawson. The only option available to them would be if Zia were married before her father and Sokolov found her. She was certain Mr. Dawson would marry her out of obligation. He was the type of gentleman who would sacrifice his own happiness to save her. She bit the inside of her lip. She would like nothing more, but she could not leg shackle him like that.

Mr. Dawson clapped his hands next to her. "I believe I have it."

Her uncle stared at Dawson. "What if she were already married before her father and the prince find her?" He looked at Zia. Had he read her thoughts? Wait, he had not offered to marry her. Only suggested she marry *someone*. "You would be safe, then, would you not?"

Heathrough sat back on the couch. "That does not seem to be a feasible plan. We have not the time. Even if we had an eligible gentleman, there is not the time for banns to be read or even a special license to be obtained before her father will arrive."

Zia purposefully avoided Mr. Dawson's gaze. "There is always Gretna," she whispered.

"I do not believe I can support such an action."

Mr. Dawson turned on the duke. "Would you prefer to see her dragged back to Russia against her will?"

Heathrough harrumphed. "The plan is for naught without a gentleman."

Tad grinned. "We need not look very far. An eligible gentleman is right here." He clapped Dawson on the back.

Heathrough narrowed his eyes at the two men. "I think not. Mr. Dawson will never be an eligible match for my niece."

Lord Munsford interjected. "This Sokolov is no gentleman, if he will treat a lady in such a brutal way. Dawson may hold no title, but he is a man of character who will protect your niece. I should think that more important than titles, Your Grace."

Her uncle took a deep, rumbling breath. "Yes, Lord Munsford. I see your point. Although, I will not admit to liking it any better, I concede it may be the only option we have."

"You all seem to have forgotten that Mr. Dawson has not expressed an interest in marrying me. I should not like to force his hand in this matter."

Dawson looked at her, concern in his eyes. "But how will that help you? I should not like to save you from one unwanted marriage by forcing you into a different one. You have much to lose by this proposition."

She closed her eyes and took a deep breath in through her nose. Slow and controlled, she filled her lungs with air. Marrying Mr. Dawson *is* what she wanted more than anything. But not like this. She wanted him to *wish* to marry her, not only to save her. "I can still run. I did it before. I should be able to do it again. I cannot let you give up your chance at happiness just to save me."

"Sokolov found you this time. He will find you again. What will he do to you if he has had to chase you that much longer? This is your best chance." He lifted her chin with his finger. "Will you consent to be my wife, Princess?" His tone was back to having the playful quality to it, as if they were sharing a joke.

She stared into his eyes and almost believed he could mean it.

Could she prevail upon his sense of kindness and honor in such a way? Would he ever be happy with her at his side? It seemed a stretch to imagine such things.

The Duke of Shearsby spoke up, pulling Zia's eyes from Mr. Dawson. "We do not have time for each of you to wonder how it will affect the other. You get on well with each other, which is more than most can boast. Mr. Dawson will be a good provider, even if it is not what you are accustomed to." He shooed them both toward the door. "Go and ready yourselves. We are to leave within the hour."

Zia coughed. "We? You are to come also?" She was to impose further on the duke and duchess as well?

"You will need a chaperone, even if you are going to be married. This will likely cause a bit of a scandal as is; we need not add to it."

Mother D. spoke for the first time since the plan was conceived. "Tad, I think it best if you remain behind with Heathrough and your wife." She looked at them all. "I can act as chaperone. I have done a fair job of it since Zia arrived at Fawn-brooke. But if Zia's father arrives here before we return, you would be in a better position to delay him further."

Shearsby shrugged and smiled. "You are prudent as ever, Mother D. I believe your plan is best." He looked to Mr. Dawson. "Take my carriage."

Mr. Dawson snorted. "As I have been borrowing it for months, I assumed I should use it this time as well."

The duke shook his head. "No. My new carriage. It is better sprung and will enable you to make better time. We can use yours until you return."

Mr. Dawson shook his head. "You are too kind, but it is not necessary."

Shearsby shook his head as he moved toward the bell pull. "Nonsense. I have made up my mind." He looked to Violet. "Will you please call for Rachel to assist with packing?" He then turned to Mr. Dawson and his mother. "You two need to do the same. Plan to meet back here in an hour. I will have Mrs. Bryse prepare some food for your journey."

They rushed from the room, but not before Mr. Dawson glanced at her over his shoulder. He furrowed his brow again, then hurried into the hallway.

Zia could not move. She should be happier about this turn of events. She would not have to leave Fawnbrooke after all. So why did she feel so dejected?

"Come, Princess. Let me help you." Zia recognized the duchess's voice. She felt herself being propelled toward the door and up the stairs to her chambers. Once inside, the duchess closed the door quietly behind her. She led Zia over to the chair by the window and fetched another chair from across the room.

Sitting knee to knee, she leaned forward and grasped Zia's hands. "I know my husband is forceful and makes plans rather quickly, but if this is not what you desire, I can sway him in another direction. You do not have to do this. You do not have to think this is your only other option besides returning with your father." Violet patted her on the knee. "I believe I know your heart, but I would like you to tell me, just the same." She pushed her chair back slightly and stood. "Think on it a moment. I shall return shortly."

Zia moved to the window seat, staring out at the silhouette of the stables.

Had it only been hours before that she had debated with herself about going to see him? And now, all of her dreams were about to come true. All, save one. In her dreams, Mr. Dawson had declared his love for her and *then* asked for her hand in marriage. The end result would be the same as she had imagined, but for one difference. She would not have his love. And was that not the most important part of all this?

She thought of the last time she had been with Prince Sokolov. Her hand went to her cheek, the sting of his hand returning. No, it was not the most important, but still very important to her. Perhaps remaining here with Mr. Dawson, safe and cared for was all she could hope at present. And she should be grateful he was the kind of man who was willing to do such a thing for her.

Violet slipped back into the room and sat on the window bench next to her. "Dawson and his mother will return shortly. What have you decided?"

"Do you think he will grow to resent me?"

"Oh, heavens no. If he is not fully in love already, I believe Dawson is at least half in love with you." She leaned forward and slipped something into Zia's hand. "But if you do not wish to go to Gretna, I will help you get away. Rose has also agreed to help."

Zia opened her hand; a roll of paper bills and a missive lay nestled there.

"It is not much, but it will get you to Rutland where Rose lives. She has written a letter of introduction for the housekeeper. It instructs her to allow you to stay as long as you need."

Zia took in a stuttering breath. "This is very kind of you—of both of you." She wiped at her nose with the back of her hand. "I think you are mistaken about Mr. Dawson's feelings for me."

The duchess smiled. "I have known Dawson for some time now. And one thing I know is even Tad cannot force him to do something he does not wish to do." She patted Zia on the arm. "He grumbles and groans much, but deep down, he is fond of the plan.

As I said, I am quite confident he more than tolerates you, Princess."

Zia wanted to believe what this woman was telling her, but she had seen his face. Had he not scowled at her as he left the room not more than an hour ago? She had heard the irritation in his voice. She knew his true feelings for her. Or did she?

Zia closed her eyes. Mr. Dawson was correct. She could not run forever. But did she have the faith to proceed with this plan?

She pressed the bills back into Violet's hand. "Thank you for this, but I will not need them. If you believe Mr. Dawson will not resent me, then I shall go through with the elopement. If not, I still have funds to get me away from Morley and my father."

"Now, Princess—"

Zia cut her off. "Please, call me Zia." She smiled, a sense of peace settling over her. "Besides, our husbands are the best of friends. Should we not be also?"

"Then I should like it if you called me Violet." Violet rubbed her forefinger along the pad of her thumb. "Are you certain you want to give all of that up?"

Zia thought about what it might mean to be married to Mr. Dawson instead of Sokolov. She nodded her head vigorously. "I should prefer to live a pauper rather than marry the likes of Prince Sokolov."

Violet seemed satisfied with Zia's answer.

Zia moved to the wardrobe. "I do not know why His Grace insisted that you help me. I have very little to pack. What I have will not take five minutes."

Violet smiled. "That is good because you have little more than ten minutes until you are to meet Dawson downstairs."

Zia's eyes flew to the clock above the mantle, verifying what Violet said to be true.

Zia pulled her valise from the bottom of the wardrobe as Lucy entered the room and Zia's chest expanded. She raced to the door and caught the girl up in an embrace before she had fully closed the door. "Oh, Lucy. I have missed you."

The girl looked befogged. "I saw you only yesterday, Princess." She took the valise from Zia's hands and moved the wardrobe, grabbing the three gowns hanging there.

"It feels like weeks." Zia caught sight of Violet and amended her words. "Not that I have been mistreated or not enjoyed my stay here at Morley. I have just missed you."

"Mr. Dawson and his mother are waiting below. They felt it best if I traveled with you to Scotland. Let us get you packed and be on our way. The skies are clear, so Mr. Dawson is hopeful we might travel well into the night before we must stop and rest the horses."

Zia nodded as Lucy placed the gowns into the valise.

Violet stood in the middle of the room. She looked as though she did not know what to do.

Zia took Violet's hands in her own. "Thank you, Violet. I am grateful to have you as a friend. I have little experience with such things. I am hopeful when I return you can show me how to be a friend in return. I was not a good one to Tiana. But I should like to change that with you."

Violet nodded. "Safe travels, Zia."

Zia's breath hitched. "Thank you."

Lucy stood at the door quietly until Zia walked toward her. "Come. We must hurry." The two of them walked quickly down the first flight of stairs, but Zia came up short when she stepped on the landing.

Mr. Dawson stood, her cloak on his arm, watching up the stairs with a stern look on his face. But when he caught sight of her, his face relaxed. He did not smile, per se, but the sides of his eyes had the slightest bit of crinkle to them. Could Violet be right? Was he not as displeased with the situation as Zia believed?

She closed her eyes for a moment and said a little prayer, asking God that Mr. Dawson would not hate her for this. She did not yet dare to ask God for Dawson's love. But if this all worked out as they planned, she resolved to ask Him for that next.

CHAPTER 21

The ride to Scotland was quiet and uneventful, albeit fast. The horses quickly put Morley Park and Leicestershire behind them. They had not had time to properly warm the bricks and even Zia's cloak could not keep the biting cold at bay for long. She sat next to Lucy on one side of the carriage while Mrs. Dawson and Mr. Dawson, Dugray—she shivered at the thought of his Christian name—sat on the opposite side. His mouth moved constantly, but little sound came out. Every now and then his scowl would deepen, and his head would offer a firm shake.

They had not even completed the task, and already he was regretting this decision. All of the previous confidence Zia had started to form crumbled down around her. By the time they had stopped to rest the horses, it was well into the night and her nerves were frazzled.

Zia stumbled from the carriage only to have Dugray reach out with his hand and steady her. "We will be within soon. I am sure you are most fatigued."

He released her and his hand raised, almost as if he were to touch her face, but to her disappointment, he dropped it back down at his side. It was the second time in a single day he had teased her with the anticipation of him touching her. She considered pulling his hand back to finish the job, but he was already handing out his mother from the carriage.

He placed a hand at the small of Zia's back and guided her inside.

A thrill shot through her until she took note that he had his hand on his mother's back also. It meant nothing. She gave herself a firm shake. She must quit trying to make every one of his movements an indication of his feelings for her. She was doing nothing but setting herself up for disappointment.

The inn was like many she had seen on her travels. It was not lavish, nor was it a hovel. It lingered somewhere lesser than the middle of both, but it was clean enough. Besides, Dugray said they would only be here for a few hours before they must set out again. They did not even let a room, only rented a private parlor and ordered some food. It seemed she had barely enough time to warm herself and they were off again into the night.

Once they were back in the carriage, Zia removed her cloak and draped it over herself and Lucy. "Perhaps if we sit close together, we can help keep each other warm." The girl looked at her oddly, but the cold soon prevailed, and she huddled close to Zia.

Zia lay her head against the window, memories of Tiana filling her mind. Before too long, her eyes grew heavy and she drifted off to sleep.

Zia awoke with a start. Mother D gave her a gentle shake. "Zia, dear, we are here. It is time to wake up."

Lucy was already out of the carriage, leaving Zia huddled under her cloak alone. She exited the carriage, the sunlight blinding her for a moment before she was able to look around. "I do not know what I expected to see in Gretna, but this is not it."

Dugray offered a small grin. "That is because this is not Gretna. We are not even in Scotland yet. It will take several more days before we reach the border." Dugray looked slightly sheepish.

The sun shone more than it had in days, even though it was covered partially by a haze of winter fog.

She stretched her arms in front of her and rounded her back to relieve the tightness. "Mother D, are your muscles not sore?"

The woman, contrary to Zia's thoughts, looked happy and well rested. How could she have sleep so comfortably?

She patted Zia on the hand. "I am well, dearest. But then, a mother can withstand much when she knows her son will be happily situated."

Zia's smile faltered. How could so many see in Dugray what she could not?

He extended his arm to her. "It is not too late to abandon this plan, if you have changed your mind." There was hope in his voice. Zia could hear it. But was he hoping they would go through with the marriage or abandon it altogether? She closed her eyes and rubbed at them on the pretense of wiping the sleep from her eyes.

In truth, she was offering a little prayer, hoping for some Divine guidance as to what she was to do. Her dreams in the carriage had been filled with her mother, and Tiana. But Dugray had been there also, disappointed and irritated with her at every encounter they had. Was this the answer she had been seeking? Were her dreams telling her not to go through with this charade?

Dugray cleared his throat and Zia's eye's popped open.

She stumbled. "No. I do not wish to change my mind, unless you do, of course."

He shook his head. "We will eat and change out the horses. Then I hope to be on our way again."

Zia emerged from the carriage, the low-hanging sun doing nothing to warm the cold air.

Dugray held his arm out to her. "This, Princess, is Gretna Green. We have finally arrived."

She had heard many tales of Gretna Green and in her mind, she had imagined there to be something grand to indicate this was the place of myths and stories. But it looked much like any other small village. Zia felt let down, as if this was an omen of some kind about the future of her marriage.

Dugray pulled her hand from his arm, dropping it to her side. She glanced at him, searching for the reason he had done so. He looked straight ahead but grabbed her hand and wrapped his fingers around hers.

Zia smiled. Perhaps there was something special about this little village after all.

He leaned down, whispering in her ear, "I will ask you one last time. Are you certain about this? Have you thought about what you are giving up if we carry on with this plan?" His brow crinkled farther than she thought possible. Nor had she believed it could be so appealing. "You do remember Fawnbrooke, do you not? It is certainly not what you are accustomed to living in."

"I have thought of nothing else but the ramifications." Was he wanting her to object, so he did not have to? Zia tilted her head. "I am fond of Fawnbrooke just the way it is. But I know you shall turn it into as grand a house as any I have seen. And I shall love it then, as well." She halted on the walkway outside the blacksmith shop. "I have no doubts about my course." Indeed, she did not. All of hers centered on the man in front of her. She knew her heart. "It is you I worry is making too hasty a decision."

He gave one firm nod of his head. "Then there is nothing left for it. Let us proceed."

Zia clenched her fist at her side, wanting to yell and stomp her foot. Why could this man give her no indication of his preference? Could he give her no clue as to his heart? Did he not see he was tearing at hers? She was convinced it would be better if he just told her he had *no* feelings for her. At least then there would be no question, no need to evaluate every word and look.

She dropped her shoulders and head. She had tried to give him an out. What more could she do?

Dugray gave her hand a squeeze and she looked up at him. His face had relaxed, his creases almost completely smoothed. Was he resigned to the decision? His demeanor seemed to say *yes*. He may not entirely hate the notion of marriage to her.

She moved closer to his side, allowing herself a tiny smile.

Dugray pulled at the door of the smithy, and Zia wrinkled her nose at the smell. Mrs. Dawson and Lucy seemed content to stay behind them, lurking just inside the door.

A young man, not much more than eighteen, stoked the fire. "May I help ye?"

Dugray cleared his throat. "We are looking for a Mr. Elliot. I understand he is an anvil priest."

"Mr. Elliot's not about the smithy, much."

Dugray frowned. "Where might we find him? We should like to be married as quickly as possible."

The young man grunted. "Doesn't everyone want it quick, sir? How much time have you on the father?" He examined Zia from her head to her feet and back again.

Dawson's jaw clenched and his hand tightened slightly around hers. Zia was not sure if it was the smell of the shop or the inferences the young man made that caused Dugray's ire. "Where might I find Mr. Elliot?"

The man hooked his thumb over his shoulder. "I should think ee's at the inn."

Dugray pulled Zia toward the door, quickly ushering her out into the early evening air.

He grunted. "I should be quite content if you should never enter that establishment again."

"But how will we marry if we do not go back?"

"Let us find this Mr. Elliot. Then we can decide if we should have to return to that place." His nose wrinkled. "It just seems so wholly—"

"Smelly?" she offered?

He grinned down at her and her breath hitched. "Yes. Precisely. It feels wrong for one's wedding to take place in such a smelly shop. But alas, if it be the place we must say our vows, then so be it." He gave her a playful nudge. "Perhaps we can just speak quickly."

This playful side of him was new to her. Was this because he was feeling closer to her, or was it for a different reason? Whatever it was, she liked it.

The foursome moved down the walkway to the inn. Dugray pulled the door open, holding it until all the women had entered. Once inside, he retook Zia's hand and led her over to the counter of the public room. He motioned to the man standing behind, wiping at a glass with a rag.

The man threw the towel over his shoulder and came to stand in front of their little group. "May I help ye?"

Dugray nodded. "We are looking for a Mr. Elliot. The boy in the smithy indicated we may find him here."

The man behind the counter smiled. What teeth he had were yellow and dotted with dark gray spots. Zia's nose scrunched up a little as his breath wafted to her. "Did yer horse throw a shoe or are ye lookin' to be married?"

Dugray raised a brow. "I do not believe it is of any concern to you, sir. If you would just be so kind as to point him out, I would be appreciative."

"If ye want me to point him out, then it be my business." The man crossed beefy arms across his even beefier chest.

Dugray huffed. "Very well. We wish to have him marry us."

The innkeeper laughed. "It is just as I suspected." He squinted at Zia. "Have ya already ruined her or does the pa be disapproving?"

Zia sucked in a breath as her mouth gaped. "How dare you insinuate that I should allow myself to be ruined."

Dugray's jaw clenched again. "Mr. Elliot, please?"

"I believe you are looking for me." Zia and Dugray turned to see a slender man standing behind them. His face was long, as was every detail upon it. Although in height, he was at least a head shorter than Dugray.

"You are Mr. Elliot, the blacksmith?"

"I am Mr. Elliot, though the boy in the smithy does more of the work than I do." The man seemed pleasant enough, unlike the man behind the counter.

Dugray looked down at Zia and squeezed her hand again.

"Had I not overheard you speaking with Mr. Jones, I should have known by watching you. You wish to be married."

Zia pulled her glance away from Dugray and shifted it to Mr. Elliot. "How would you have known that was to be our request?"

He chuckled. "It is quite evident, I assure you." He twitched his lips. "And rather refreshing. It is usually only the lassies that have the look of calf-love. But it is quite obvious the gentleman here is not only after your money, miss."

Zia was not sure whether to be flattered or offended. But she had little time to be either as Mr. Elliot ushered them into a private parlor and pulled the curtain closed behind them. Zia raised a brow. It was obvious they were not the first to seek out Mr. Elliot here.

Mr. Elliot held out his hand. "There is a small matter about my fee. Will you be wanting the full service? It does include a room upstairs, should you be needing it."

Dugray shook his head, his ears turning pink as he handed over the money. "There will be no need for a room. Just a quick service, please. Can we proceed? I should like to be on our way back as soon as possible."

Elliot chuckled again. "Yes, it is always better to be gone before the father arrives."

He glanced back at Mrs. Dawson and Lucy. "Be they your witnesses?"

Zia and Dugray nodded their heads in unison. "And what be your names?"

"Dugray Charles Dawson and—" he looked to Zia.

She smiled up at him. "Zia Natalya Catherine Petrovich."

"Then let us continue." Mr. Elliot assumed a most pious look and pose as he looked down his long nose at Zia. "Miss Zia Natalya Catherine Petrovich, are you here willingly and do you wish to be married to this man?"

Zia swallowed. This was it. This was the last chance for them to change their minds. She had no desire to do so, but given the chance, would Dugray? She licked her lips. "Yes."

He asked the same questions of Dugray, and Zia's muscles tensed.

"Yes," he said resolutely.

Air flooded from her lungs. Surely, he would not go back on the marriage now.

"We are off to a good start then, are we not?" Mr. Elliot

clapped his hands together. "Just a few more minutes and you shall be officially married."

Dugray looked at the man with wide eyes. "Yes. Please, carry on."

Mr. Elliot leaned toward Dugray. "Are you sure about the room, sir?

Dugray clenched his jaw tightly. "Quite sure. Now please continue."

Mr. Elliot shrugged and cleared his throat. "Miss Zia Natalya Catherine Petrovich, will you take Mr. Dugray Charles Dawson as your lawfully wedded husband?"

Zia nodded. "I will."

Mr. Elliot nodded. "Good. Good. And will you, Mr. Dugray Charles Dawson take Miss Zia Natalya Catherine Petrovich as your lawfully wedded wife?"

Dugray looked down at her. There was no crease in his fore-head, nor downturned lips. Indeed, he looked quite at peace. "I most certainly do."

Zia's heart lurched. His response indicated a degree of deter-mination and resolve, perhaps even happiness. It gave her hope.

Mr. Elliot produced rings from his pocket.

"You have rings at the ready? How often do you perform such ceremonies?" Dugray looked at him questioningly.

"I find it best to always be prepared. One knows not when they will be called upon." He handed a ring to each of them. "Repeat after me, Mr. Dawson. 'With this ring I thee wed, with my body I thee worship, and with all my worldly goods I thee endow.'"

Dugray repeated it and placed the ring on Zia's fourth finger. It hung loosely there.

It was then her turn. She repeated after Mr. Elliot, but when she went to put the ring on Dugray's finger, she could not slide it past the first knuckle.

Mr. Elliot shrugged. "I cannot fit everyone. It is more of a general size." He then joined their hands together. "Those whom God hath joined together let no man put asunder."

Was this man inferring he was acting on God's behalf? It was odd, to be sure, but it did make the ceremony feel a bit more like a church wedding. Zia glanced at Dugray from the corner of her eye. His lips twitched slightly, and she felt hers do the same.

Mr. Elliot took a step back and with a flourish of his hands and a bow, he shouted, "I pronounce that you be man and wife together."

Dawson and Zia stood there, neither seeming to understand what they should do next.

Mr. Elliot leaned forward and whispered loudly to Dugray. "If you will not be using the room, perhaps you should, at the very least, kiss your bride."

Zia's heart raced. Was he going to do it? She both wished for it and dreaded it. In her mind, the first time he kissed her would be private, not here on display for anyone choosing to poke their head through the curtain. But if this was her only chance to kiss him, she did not wish to waste it.

She did not dare look directly at him, knowing he would see what she wanted. He would certainly think her wanton.

Zia felt him shift. Was he going to kiss her? He leaned forward and brushed a kiss to her cheek and disappointment flooded through her. He did not desire her. Everything she thought she had seen in his face during the ceremony she had mistaken.

But he did not pull back immediately. One hand still held tightly onto hers, while his other came up and cupped her cheek.

Her breath stuttered from her throat.

"I should like our first kiss to be private, not on display for this popinjay."

She swallowed and gave a slight nod. He *did* want to kiss her. Zia thought she might just float from the room, so light she felt.

Mr. Elliot grunted. "All that is left is for all of you to sign the certificate."

CHAPTER 22

He had done it. He had married Zia. Not exactly over the blacksmith's anvil, but close enough. Should he not feel only happiness with this situation? Was it not what he had desired most?

He sighed. No. Her love was what he desired most, and he could not be certain he had that. Perhaps in time it would come; for now, he could at least boast he was less objectionable than a black hearted prince.

Zia seemed resigned to the idea that they were now man and wife, but he had seen her frown when he had leaned to brush a kiss to her cheek. He had told her he preferred a more private setting, but would she allow it to happen at all?

He glanced over at her huddled up in the corner of the bench. Her head was turned away from him, but Dawson could tell from her breathing she was not asleep. She chose to pretend rather than speak with him?

If he shifted over several hands, his leg could rest against hers. His mother had insisted that now they were married, they should sit next to each other. Dawson had embraced the idea, but Zia had only shrugged and scooted to the far side of the carriage.

He grunted.

She had been quiet for most of the afternoon. She shifted slightly and he could see her eyes were open as she watched the scenery fly by. Dusk was casting a pink hue over the landscape. It was breathtaking and yet, Dawson could not pull his eyes away from his bride. *Bride.* Would it ever feel normal to call her such?

What was she thinking?

Surely, she regretted the whole affair. The ceremony in a dirty private parlor could not have been the wedding of Zia's dreams. But surely it was at least better than the dirty, smelly smithy they had first encountered.

The urge to move closer to her pounded in his chest. What would she do if he closed the distance? Dawson looked across the carriage at Zia's maid and his mother. Both the women appeared to be asleep. While the maid's head lolled from side to side, his mother sat upright, with her head laid back against the bench.

Pushing aside his apprehensions, Dawson scooted closer to his wife. He swallowed hard at that thought. *His wife.* All these terms felt foreign to him.

He put his hand on the bench and it brushed against her thigh. She flinched and he pulled it back, resting it on *his* thigh. His frown intensified.

He knew Prince Sokolov was a violent man. The many times Zia had flinched at his touch verified the stories she told. Dawson sighed deeply. He had saved her from such a fate, at the very least. He would take consolation in that fact.

Zia sat up, looking down at the closeness of his leg to hers, then turned her gaze up to meet his. Should he move back? She did not look angry, so perhaps she was not opposed to the closeness. He clasped his hands in his lap. Had he not held her hand through the entirety of their stay in Gretna? Why was he hesitant to hold it now?

"Are you warm enough?" He was glad he had picked the deep burgundy wool for her cloak, as it brought out the red highlights in her dark brown hair.

She nodded, running a hand over the fabric. "I do not think I ever properly thanked you for this."

He shrugged. "You have little to thank me for. The cloak was already yours. And the warmest part is still the same."

She shook her head. "But I was unable to wear it; it did not matter if it was mine or not. You are the one who changed it. You made it so I could no longer see Tiana in it."

"I am happy I could provide you with some warmth." His voice was stilted and formal. Tad would surely find the situation wholly amusing. Should he not be able to converse more casually now that they had much of the strictures of society lifted?

She watched him for a moment and then turned back to the window. Silence permeated the carriage.

"Do you miss Russia? Does this weather lend to a longing for home?" Is that why she chose not to talk to him—because she was homesick?

Gah. Why did he not leave her in peace? Surely she desired it more than speaking with him of nonsensical things.

She shrugged. "When I first came here, I missed my home. But when I think back on it, there is little there for me since my mother died."

"But what of your family? Do you not have brothers or sisters? And what of your father? Surely you will miss seeing him." He ran a hand though his hair. "When the estate is in a better position, I will see we take a trip to visit." He cleared his throat. "Unless you would prefer to go alone."

She watched him for a moment. "You are a good, kind man,

Mr. Dawson. But if we do not return to Odessa, it shall be no matter. I can be contented here. And no. I do not have any brothers or sisters."

She sighed and stared at him a moment. "I think it is my father's greatest regret, having no heir." She put her hand on the bench between them and shifted on her seat to face him more fully; she did not lift her hand back into her lap once she was situated.

Should he place his hand atop hers? Is that what she wished him to do? Or had she not realized her hand still rested there? Should he not have a better knowledge of women at his age? Gah. He was a completely love-sick dolt.

He could think on the matter until they arrived home and have nothing come of it. How would he know her feelings if he never took the risk? She had not removed her hand, so it was possible she would not do so now.

Taking a deep breath, Dawson placed his hand on top of hers, turning slightly toward her. She did not snatch her hand back or scold him. His chest expanded as he curled his fingers around hers.

She glanced down at their hands, and he doubted himself; but she not only kept her hand under his, she turned it over and intertwined their fingers. *Oh.* If he did not die of apoplexy before this journey was over, it would be a miracle.

"I am sure your father is pleased with you." Was that his voice? It was at least an octave higher than normal. "You do not think he loves you less because you are not a boy, do you?"

"I think it is natural for a man to wish for a son to carry on his title and inherit his estates. Do you not agree, Mr. Dawson?"

He shrugged. "Where I come from, an educated, healthy girl is every bit as desirable as a boy. But there are not the inheritance laws as here in England." He glanced out the window, realizing she may ask more about America. He was not sure he was ready for that conversation yet. "It is likely your father will already be at Morley when we return. Are you afraid to see him?" At least his voice was returning to its normal timbre.

Zia rubbed at her earlobe. "No. Apprehensive is a more accurate word."

Dawson had wondered about Zia's father and his character. Was he cruel, as the prince obviously was? And if he was not, why would he have his only daughter marry such a man?

"My father is a good man. He was kind and caring when I was a child. But when my mother died, he withdrew. He was not often at home, preferring to spend his time in St. Petersburg or Moscow." She sighed. "He will be angry with me for running away. But he will forgive me—in time."

"But will he forgive you for marrying another man? And one so decidedly below your station?"

Zia shrugged. "He will not have a choice. It is done and there is nothing for him to do about it now." She fiddled with his fingers and he smiled. "It is Prince Sokolov whom I fear. He will not forgive me for marring his reputation." She held his gaze. "Thank you for protecting me, Mr. Dawson."

Dawson bit the inside of his cheek. Did he dare take this further so quickly? He had only just held her hand. But what was the saying? In for a penny, in for a pound? He plunged ahead. "We are man and wife now. In America it is not uncommon for married couples to use Christian names." He glanced at her. Would she object to him calling her Zia even though he had been doing it in his mind for some time?

She nodded. "But I thought you did not like to be called Dugray. Your mother told me only she is allowed to call you by that name."

Dawson closed his eyes. It was because no one ever said it the way Zia did. The slight twirl of her tongue when she said the *g* and *r* together was like nothing he had ever heard. And it warmed him thoroughly. "I believe I could get used to you using it." There was the squeak in his voice again.

"Very well, Dugray. I admit I prefer it to Mr. Dawson."

Was it calling him Mr. Dawson she did not like or was it the name in general? She likely regretted having no title affixed to her name.

As if sensing his question, she continued. "And while I like the sound of Mrs. Dawson, that is your mother. Between you and I, Zia would be more desirable." She looked up at him from under her lashes. "Although, others may not call me princess anymore, I admit to growing accustomed to you calling me such."

Dawson's shoulders relaxed and a smile hovered on his lips. "By English law, you are able to retain your title. I should think many will call you princess."

She looked at him and his breath stopped. "But it is only you I desire to hear it from." She scooted closer to him but looked out the window. "Where exactly is it you are from, Dugray? I believe you told me you were born in America?"

He nodded. "Yes. I was born in Pennsylvania. My father's family has lived there since his parents helped settle the land with William Penn."

Her brow furrowed. "I know not of this William Penn."

Dawson grinned. She looked quite appealing when her face was scrunched up in thought. "He was the founder and settler of the state of Pennsylvania. He received the land from Charles the Second as repayment of a debt the King owed Penn's father." He settled back against the bench, pulling her hand with his and setting it on his leg. Her eyes widened slightly, but still she kept it entwined with his. "My grandfather was a Quaker, like Penn, and fled persecution here in England. Penn allowed many of his Quaker friends to purchase land within his holdings."

She looked at him. "Then how were you able to return here? Are the Quakers still not persecuted?"

Dawson shrugged. "Not as much as in the past. But it is no matter. My father abandoned the Quaker life when he reached his majority."

"And he was still able to live among the other Quakers? That did not cause problems?"

"Some, perhaps, but his father had purchased the land. William Penn was an advocate for religious freedom. He never placed restrictions stating people must be Quakers to live in Pennsylvania. Quakers, by virtue of their religion, are a peaceful people. They would not have driven nonbelievers away."

Zia's eyes began to droop. The sun was nearly below the horizon now and after the lateness of the previous nights, Dawson's own eyes burned and ached. "You look tired." He took off his greatcoat and folded it up into a square, placing it at his shoulder. "You may lie against me to sleep if that would suit you. I am certain leaning against the side of the carriage will only succeed in cricking your neck and making you colder."

She rubbed her hand over his coat. "But you will be cold without your coat."

He shook his head, unable to tell her that just looking at her heated him through. "I am warm enough. You need not worry."

She waved him aside and stood up enough to pull her cloak out from under her. "I think we can share this; do you not agree?"

He opened his mouth to protest, but she held up her hand.

"I will brook no protests. You will use the cloak, or I shall not sleep."

He nodded and she smiled as she fanned it out until it settled around them both.

His chest squeezed and he knew he would do whatever she asked of him, just so he could see her smile. *Lud. I love her.* He ached. Both because he loved her so deeply and because he doubted she could ever return the depth of his feelings.

She snuggled into him, putting an arm around his middle in order to make less space between them so that the cloak would fully cover them both. "Are you comfortable or shall I move my arm?"

He could not speak, only shake his head and place his arm on top of hers. A contented sigh left her lips and her eyes fluttered shut.

The weariness left his eyes as he watched Zia fall asleep. When her breathing settled into a deep, even rhythm, he lifted his arm off hers, tracing his finger along her cheek bone and jaw. He lightly ran his thumb over her eyelids, loving the feel of her soft lashes.

His eyes dropped and he lightly ran his finger along the contour of her top lip. They were supple to the touch. What would it be like to kiss her? He did not dare attempt it when she was awake. But was it wrong to do it when she was asleep, when she could not voice her objection beforehand? He held his breath, fighting every impulse inside him that told him to do it anyway.

"I will not object if you kiss me." Her whispered voice sounded as if it was being trumpeted from the rooftops. His head jerked up as she opened one eye.

He stared down at her, his mouth slightly parted. Had she really spoken, or had he imagined it?

"You are not going to make me ask again, are you, Dugray?"

He shook his head and bent slightly, his lips finding hers without the use of sight in the darkening carriage. He brushed his lips lightly against hers. She tasted like honey and black currents.

He pulled back as her body twitched next to him.

Reaching up a hand, she placed it behind his neck, slowly drawing him back down to her. She took control of the kiss, firmly moving her lips over his until he took over again.

He sighed against her cheek, trying to catch his breath coming in hungry gulps.

He was vaguely aware that his mother and Zia's maid sat on the opposite bench. But he did not wish to think on them in this moment. He only wanted Zia.

Her fingers twirled through the hair at the back of his neck. He had been meaning to have it trimmed, but now he thought himself very fortunate for having not taken the time. "What are you doing to me, Zia?" He barely recognized the voice coming from his mouth.

She let out a quiet gasp. "Say it again."

"What are you doing to me?"

She pulled back slightly. "No. Say my name. It is the first I have heard you say it aloud."

"Zia."

She ran her fingers over the lines permanently etched into his forehead from years of scowling. His body tensed and then relaxed, his mouth settling into a soft smile.

"I will say it as many times as you ask."

She smiled up into his face. Her hand left his hair and came to rest on his cheek, her thumb rubbing along the stubble on his jaw. "I find myself at odds with your mother, Dugray."

He raised a brow. "Pray, how so?"

"I love to see your face, but I find I quite like your beard, as well."

He grinned down at her. "After this journey, I believe you shall have your wish, Zia."

"Then I shall be content." She sighed and rested her head against him.

"But will you stay content?" He put voice to greatest fears.

She turned her gaze up to him. "If I am with you, I could not be anything but happy." Zia wrapped her arm around his middle and laid down on his chest.

Using his free hand, he tried his best to rearrange the cloak around them. "Sleep well, Princess." He dropped a kiss onto the top of her head, his eyes closing at last. He no longer felt the ache and longing from moments ago. All he felt was hope and happiness.

CHAPTER 23

The journey back to Fawnbrooke was one of the most enjoyable Zia could recall. After three days of sharing her cloak with Dugray, even when the bricks were fresh and hot, she'd never felt so close to him. But when the carriage finally turned onto the pebbled drive of Fawnbrooke, she was both relieved and nervous to be home. The afternoon sunlight reflected off the windows of the manor house, giving the exterior a golden hue.

She ran her tongue over her lips, still feeling the warmth left by Dugray's many kisses. She would never have guessed a passionate man lived beneath the scowls and glares. Granted, she had been the one to act in a most untoward way but Zia felt it was worth it when she discovered what he had been hiding all this time. She could feel no remorse for her actions.

She loved this man and she now believed he loved her too. He could not kiss her in such a manner if he did not love her, could he? She did not believe it possible. But she knew little of men and as the carriage traveled up the drive, that notion wormed a small amount of doubt into her head.

Sleeping within his arms had been pure bliss, but now that they were home, a shyness settled over her. In the quiet of the carriage, when Lucy and his mother had been sleeping, they had stolen kisses and whispered endearments. But now, they were home and things felt different. *Home.* It hardly seemed possible.

Zia stepped from the carriage, looking at the house with new eyes. The eyes of a mistress. She was mistress of this estate and with it came a sort of protectiveness. She remembered the first time she had awakened in this house. Heat colored her cheeks as she remembered the disdain she had shown these people who had so kindly rescued her and taken her in. She barely recognized the girl in those memories.

Dugray let go of her hand and she frowned, until she saw him hand his mother, and even Lucy from the carriage. Once both women were safely on the ground and Lucy was on her way to the servants' entrance, he took her hand again, tucking it securely into the crook of his arm.

"What do you think of her, Princess? Perhaps you now regret your decision?" He looked down at her, almost as if he were having the same hesitations as she. Could he be worrying about their new life together? Could he wonder what her feelings were after what had happened in the carriage? It seemed preposterous. Yet had she not doubted his?

They reached the doorway and he held her back, allowing his mother to enter first. When Mother D was through the door, he bent and swung Zia up into his arms.

She let out a squeal. "Dugray, what are you doing?"

He grinned down at her. "Where I come from, it is customary to protect a bride from the evil spirits which may be lurking about the entryway floor of her new home. Besides, what if you should trip walking over the threshold? Such would not bode well for our marriage. I cannot take such a risk."

His eyes crinkled at the corners and Zia rubbed her thumb over one side. She knew she would do anything in her power to make him happy so she could see those crinkles often.

Dugray set her down and stepped away. The house felt much warmer now than it had before she left for Morley Park with her uncle. Could it be the difference between being a guest and a mistress? Whatever it was, she did not care. She was married to the man she loved, and this was their home. They would raise their children within these walls. The thought of having children with Dugray brought gooseflesh to her skin.

Mrs. Hardy bustled in from the small room to the side. Two maids were busily polishing a stack of silver.

Dugray took several steps forward. "Mrs. Hardy, where did the silver come from? I do not remember having any before we left for Gretna."

"No, sir. I should think you did not." She shot a nervous glance at Mother D. "Your larger trunks were delivered while you were away, ma'am. While I was unpacking your things, I found this silver tucked among your gowns and stockings. I hope you do not mind that I took the liberty of polishing it up for you."

Mother D shook her head. "Not at all, Mrs. Hardy." She put her hand on Dugray's other arm. "It was my father's silver. We received it as a part of my trousseau at our marriage. Your father left you with little else. I thought you should have it here at your home."

Dugray stepped out of his mother's and Zia's grasp. He ducked into the small room and collected a spoon off the table, examining it closely. "How did he not gamble this away as well?"

Mother D shrugged. "I may have given him the impression that the silver had already been sold." She looked at him unrepentantly. "If he had known we were still in possession of it, you would have had nothing."

"Why did you not sell it after he died? I am certain you could have used the blunt it would have fetched, Mother."

She shook her head. "It was not mine to sell, Dugray. It was always meant to be yours."

Zia walked over, stopping next to Dugray. She picked up a fork, seeing the intricate letter *G* engraved into the silverware for his mother's maiden name of Greene. "It is lovely."

Mrs. Hardy stood anxiously in the doorway.

Dugray put the spoon back on the table. "I shall leave you to your work." He bowed his head and turned to leave the room.

"I have also seen to it that Her Highness's things be moved to the mistress's chambers that adjoin yours, sir."

Zia's cheeks warmed. "I'm sure it was a very quick move, indeed."

"Thank you, Mrs. Hardy. You are efficient, as always." Dugray glanced at Zia.

Mrs. Hardy followed his gaze, looking keenly at her new mistress. "I believe, ma'am, you will find your new wardrobe quite full of gowns and slippers."

Zia frowned and looked at Dugray. "You should not have purchased so much. I do not need many gowns. I have enjoyed our simple life."

Dugray held up his hands. "It was not I. Although, seeing that surprised twinkle in your eyes, I am sorry it was not."

She turned to Mrs. Hardy. "If it was not my husband, then who?"

"I believe you will find a card on your dressing table, miss." Mrs. Hardy curtsied. "I should be checking out the polishers. They are new to the job. Good day, ma'am. Mr. Dawson, sir."

Zia took a step away from her husband, suddenly shy as to

what would come next. "You must have business that requires your attention after our long absence." There was a pout to her voice, but she did not care. She was not anxious to give up the closeness they had shared in the carriage for the last three days.

Dugray shrugged. "There is nothing that cannot wait another day, I am sure." He stepped closer to her. Dipping his head down, he placed a light kiss on her lips.

She shivered at both his closeness and the breath tickling her neck. "I had thought to read, but I find my legs are in need of stretching. I thought I may take a turn."

"Do you seek solitude, or might I impose and join you?"

Zia wrapped her hands around the crook of his arm. "I could hope for nothing more."

Dugray retrieved her cloak and his greatcoat. He had just finished pushing his gloves onto each finger when the knocker on the door sounded.

One of the maids from the silver polishing rushed to the door.

"Is Mr. Dawson home yet? I thought I saw my carriage return to the carriage house."

Zia recognized Shearsby's voice. Although, she had never heard the strain that was in it now.

The maid opened the door wider and the duke's eyes widened when he spotted Dugray.

"Ah, Dawson. You are back." He looked between Zia and Dugray. "And I assume your journey was successful?"

Dawson grinned and took Zia's hand, raising it to his lips. "Yes. Zia and I are now married."

The duke clapped Dugray on the back and offered a bow to Zia. "I am happy to hear it. And your timing could not have been better." He shifted his gaze to Zia. "Your father and Prince Sokolov arrived just yesterday." He cleared his throat awkwardly.

"They were not pleased to find you were not about when they finally tracked Heathrough to Morley."

Zia's hands tightened in Dugray's. "They are here?"

Tad nodded. "Your father, though irritated, seems to be a nice enough gentleman." He raised his brows. "But your Sokolov? I should not like to see my nemesis's leg shackled to that man."

Zia raised her chin. "He is not *my* Sokolov."

Dugray pulled his hand from her grip and slid it around her waist, pulling her closer to him. "Do they know we have returned?"

Shearsby shook his head. "No, but I should think it will not be long before they are aware."

"Do they know of the marriage?"

Zia was content to let Dugray ask all the questions that were bouncing around in her head.

The duke's eyes widened. "That is a bee's hive I did not wish to disturb. Besides, I was not certain you would both follow through."

Dugray growled. "And why should you have thought that?"

The bland expression on the duke's face would have made Zia laugh, were she not so worried. "You really need ask? There was so much concern, on both sides, that the other did not feel as you did. I was certain one of you would have abandoned the idea to save the other from a life of misery and woe." His voice was devoid of any enthusiasm. "Which would have, of course, been very absurd."

Dugray ran a hand across the back of his neck. "I feel as though we need to make a plan before Zia is forced to face Prince Sokolov." He looked down at her. "You need not be so frightened, Princess. I shall not let anything happen to you."

Looking up into his eyes, Zia could almost believe anything was possible. He set her at ease. If he was by her side, she thought she might just be able to survive this encounter.

"I believe we should go immediately. The sooner I face Sokolov, the sooner he may return to Russia and leave us in peace."

He rubbed small circles on her hip bone with his thumb. Her heart pulsed to the rhythm he created. "Are you sure? I think it better if we have a strategy."

She shook her head. "No. I wish to go now."

CHAPTER 24

P rince Sokolov stood in front of the fireplace, his back to
the room. But Zia would recognize his slightly hunched
form anywhere. It had haunted enough of her dreams to
never be fully erased from her memory.

She took a step back into the corridor. A warm, steadying hand
settled around her waist. She closed her eyes, relishing in his
touch. His slight pressure pushed her to take the steps back into
the room.

Her father was seated on the sofa, his arm draped across the
back, his leg crossed over the other at the knee. He turned toward
her when she entered the room.

Zia expected him to be angry or worse when she saw him
again but was surprised to see a smile turn up his lips when his
gaze settled on her. He rose to his feet and met her at the center of
the room.

"*Samyy dorogoy,*" he said in Russian. "Dearest. You are looking
well. The English air has been good for you. After hearing of your
accident, I feared for the worst. But I am pleased to see that you

are still pretty enough." He turned her to the side and examined the narrow scar running from her hairline onto her cheek. "I see no reason why Sokolov should cast you aside and forego the marriage."

Zia put a hand to her cheek. She had not thought on that scar in weeks. She shook head. "No, Papa. Did you not read the letter I left when I fled? I will not marry him."

Her father waved her away. "You can and you will. It is just the nerves of a young girl." He gave his fingers a snap and waved Sokolov over to them. "Now you will apologize to Prince Sokolov for all the trouble you have caused and then we shall be on our way. We have both been away far too long."

Prince Sokolov joined the small grouping, standing in front of Zia and Dugray. Both Shearsby and Heathrough joined them also.

Zia took a step away from Sokolov. "I cannot marry him, Papa." She jutted out her chin, refusing to shrink before him ever again.

"And I say you can. You are a silly girl. I believed you to have more brains in your head. Apparently, I have indulged you far too much. You will now do as you are told." Her father reached forward to grip her arm.

Dugray intercepted and grabbed a hold of her father's hand before he could touch Zia. "She will not marry the Prince, because she is already married to me. In England, a lady may only have one husband."

Zia looked at him, surprised at the easy way he spoke Russian. She knew he understood some—a little by his account—but he had never said how well he could speak it.

Her father and Sokolov glared down at her, convincing her to think on Dugray and his Russian at a later time. "What is this man speaking about?"

Zia clasped her hands behind her back, twisting them about

until her skin burned. "He is in earnest, Papa. We were married a few days ago, at Gretna Green."

Dugray's hand moved between hers, ending the torture she was inflicting upon them, and intertwined her fingers with his.

She took a deep breath, willing his courage into her. "Had I known you were coming, I should have waited and allowed you to attend the ceremony." It was a bold lie, but she did not care. She felt in control of her life at last.

Her father sputtered for a moment and Sokolov seared her with his angry glare. He was the first to speak. He flicked his chin in Dugray's direction. "And who is this...man? Is he worthy of your title? Of your heritage? You are the great granddaughter of the Great Tzar Peter."

The Duke of Shearsby stepped forward. "Perhaps I should have made introductions sooner. This is Mr. Dugray Dawson. His estate is located not far from here."

Her father laughed. "Mr.? He has not even a lowly title, Zia? How could you align yourself with someone so inferior? This is not to be tolerated." He turned on Heathrough. "How could you have allowed this to happen. I thought you were to look after her while she was in your country?"

Zia's father turned to Sokolov. "I shall have the annulment papers drawn up immediately." He turned to Sokolov, his head shaking. "This will delay our return by several days, perhaps even a week. But there is nothing for it."

Zia felt all her control slipping away. Would Dugray not say anything? Would he not object to the annulment? Could it be he was having second thoughts on the marriage now that he was faced with Sokolov and her father?

Zia shook her head, trying to rid her mind of the damaging thoughts. She did not care. Whatever he was thinking, they could figure it all out in time. For now, she needed to speak. She needed to regain control of her life.

"No!" she shouted. All conversation stopped and all eyes turned on her. Sokolov's gaze was narrow and cold, while Dugray's held warmth and a hint of—dare she believe it—hope. "No. There will be no annulment. I am married to Dugray and I will be remaining in England with Dugray." She took in a lungful of air through her nose. "There can be no annulment if the marriage has been consummated." She bit down hard on the inside of her cheek. All Dugray's prrevious assumptions of her were now coming to fruition. Lie after lie seemed to fall from her lips. Only, now her lies involved him. He must surely be regretting his decision to marry her now.

Her father turned on her. "And have you?" Her face heated to discuss such matters in such a public display, but the color seemed to convince her father of the truthfulness of her words.

Sokolov swore in Russian.

"Why would you lower yourself to marry such a man, Zia?" You had your choice of suitors in Russia. I do not understand your decisions."

"He is a gentleman, Father. He has a good living." She swallowed as discreetly as possible. She had become a true proficient. And now that she was so proficient, would Dugray believe what she said next? "And I love him, Father."

Her father stopped his whispered conversation with Sokolov and turned to look at her, his gaze suddenly appraising her in a new way.

"You understand marrying for love, Papa. I know you do. Please, let me have what you and Mama had." Zia took a deep, shuddering breath. She had said it. He had not declared his love for her, but she had felt him suck in a breath. Was it because he felt the same or because he did not? Whatever the cause, she did not regret her words. She should have told him before now her feelings, rather than assuming he knew them already. And whether he felt it as well or not, Zia was sure this was the only course of action which would sway her father from his current path.

"I was protecting you from pain, child. Love hurts when you lose it." Her father took a step toward her. His fingers stroked at his chin as he glanced between Zia and Dugray. His brow furrowed. "You do love him. I can see it in your eyes," he said to Zia. "Why could you not have loved a man of title?" He gave her a small smile, then shook his head and looked closer at them both. Tilting his head, he took note of their clasped hands. "And you love my daughter, do you not?"

Dugray nodded and cleared his throat. "More than I ever thought possible, Your Highness."

Zia's stomach fluttered about and her heart hammered hard and quick. He loved her? She had hoped it to be true. Allowed herself to imagine it. But deep down she was afraid it could not be true.

She looked up at him through her lashes and her knees weakened. How had she not seen it there before? Now that she knew his feelings, it was so obviously there in the look he gave her. She realized now it had been there for days, perhaps even weeks. She could not put her finger on exactly when he had begun to look on her in such a way, but it did not matter. He looked on her now with such love and respect. *That* is what mattered.

Prince Petrovich turned to Sokolov. "What of you, Sokolov? Do you love my daughter?"

Sokolov gave a laugh-sneer. "Of course, I love her. Would I have traveled all this way to get her if I did not?" He pounded his fist into his other hand. "What is all this talk of love? You have become weak. Are you going to let a woman make us look the fool?"

"You do not need my help for that, Your Highness." Zia knew she was provoking Sokolov, but she needed her father to believe what she had told him in her letter.

Sokolov raised his hand, quickly bringing it down toward her face. Zia flinched, waiting for the impact, but Dugray reached out and tightly gripped the man's wrist before he could complete the action. Dugray gave him a small push backwards.

Zia's father's brows raised before they settled into a squint. He stared at Sokolov for a long, quiet moment.

Sokolov squirmed under the scrutiny.

Petrovich sighed. "I believe you traveled all this way to get her dowry. The addition of her land with yours will more than double your holdings. Do not think me ignorant, Sokolov."

Prince Sokolov glared at Zia and her father. "We had a bargain. You made promises to me. I have already made plans— paid out large sums of money based on those promises."

Her father shrugged. "Your business dealings are not my concern." He smiled at Zia, though it was tinged with sadness. "What is it your mother used to say, child? 'A bird in the hand is worth two in the bush.'" He turned to Sokolov. "Your birds were still in the bush."

He turned to Zia and cast a glance at Dugray. "Does he treat you with respect, child?"

Zia nodded and leaned into Dugray. He wrapped his arm around her waist.

Petrovich sighed and clapped a hand on Dugray's shoulder. "Take good care of her, sir."

Dugray nodded. "I shall endeavor to do so every day of my life, Your Highness."

"I shall not stand for this," Sokolov said. "When she is a widow there shall be nothing preventing me from taking her back to Russia." Sokolov lunged at Dugray.

Zia screamed as the two men tumbled to the floor, Sokolov's hands trying to strangle Dugray.

Pride welled up inside Zia as Dugray maneuvered out from under the prince and managed to pin him to the floor. He pulled his arm back, ready to strike when Shearsby and her father hurried over, grasping hold of Dugray and hauling him off of Sokolov. "I know you desire to pummel the man, Dawson. But it will only serve to make your hand hurt. It would be a pity if you were unable to hold your wife's hand because you chose to land this gentleman a facer." Shearsby held tightly to Dawson's arms.

Dugray yanked his arms free, returning to Zia's side. She put her hand to his cheek. "Are you injured?"

He shook his head. "No. But I worry for you as long as this man is freely roaming about England."

Her father stepped forward and put out a hand to help Sokolov from the floor. "I shall see this gentleman makes it back to Russia. You need not worry about him." He glared at Sokolov, but then turned his gaze on Zia. "I shall miss you, daughter."

"And I you, Papa. This is not goodbye forever. Dugray has promised we can visit Odessa in time."

Her father nodded. "I should like that very much. But before then, I shall return to England and personally deliver the proceeds from the sale of your land. I assume you would like to have the money instead?"

Zia looked at Dugray and she knew immediately that he would wish her to keep it. When had she learned his thoughts? "Perhaps we can discuss it and send you word of our desires?"

Her father nodded. "We have trespassed on Shearsby long enough. We must be taking our leave. Sokolov." He gave the man a push toward the door.

"I cannot return with nothing," he spat out. "What am I to do about my creditors?"

"I fear there is little you can do about it here in the country, Sokolov. Perhaps you can find an heiress or someone with a healthy dowry in London. Someone willing to marry you in exchange for a title." Shearsby grinned. "The English do love the title of *princess*."

Sokolov's brows creased, as if he were truly considering the notion. But he could not be in earnest, could he?

Zia gave an internal shrug. What did she care? She would remain with Dugray at Fawnbrooke and that was all that mattered.

Her father looked around the room. "I confess. I have no desire to return to London. And the Atlantic is surely to be tumultuous. My estate is well in hand for several months yet." He looked to Zia, his brows raised. "Perhaps I could impose on my daughter and her husband, rather than the kindness of the Duke of Shearsby."

The duke stepped forward. "It is no imposition, Your Highness, but I should understand your desire to be with your daughter. Please know the invitation to stay at Morley Park is always open."

"As is Chatney House." The Duke of Heathrough clapped Zia's father on the shoulder.

Zia glanced at Dugray and then Shearsby. "Perhaps my father could stay on here at Morley at least until the morrow, to enable us to prepare his room at Fawnbrooke."

What could they possibly do in a day's time? Her father would soon know of her deceit. But she did not care. Dugray would convince her father of the eventual success of Fawnbrooke, as he did everyone he told of it.

Zia did not believe that when her father learned of the state of

Fawnbrooke that he would reconsider Sokolov's pursuit of her. Not now that he had seen the man's true nature.

Her only reservation was Sokolov himself. Could he be trusted to stay in London? It should not surprise her if he should come and try to kill Dugray in his sleep.

Shearsby watched her closely, giving her a nod and a wink when she caught his gaze.

Dugray shook his head. "Nonsense. We will make room for him now." She looked up at him, her mouth pulled down into a frown. "But..."

He pulled her gently to the side and dropped his forehead onto hers. "From here on out, no more lies, no more deceit. Your father agreed to this marriage because we love each other. Unless that was also a lie—"

Zia shook her head. "No. That was the complete truth."

Dugray smiled. "I am happy to hear it. The lie about the money will, I am sure, make him leery. But more lies and secrecy will only make that worse. I will show him about Fawnbrooke and tell him of our plans, show him what we have already done. He will see that I am good on my word."

Zia cupped his face in both of her hands. "You are right."

Dugray's smile grew as he looked into her eyes. "Yes, Princess. I usually am." He put his finger under her chin and lifted it slightly. Her eyes fluttered closed and her breath halted in her throat.

He brushed a soft kiss over her lips, and she leaned into him. He pulled away and she placed her hands on his coat, her fingers curling around the lapels.

"We will do this together." He bent down and whispered in her ear. "All of this." The whisper became tiny kisses just below her ear. Zia giggled as Dugray grudgingly pulled away.

Zia reached out to a nearby chair to steady herself, her breath coming out jumpy and uneven.

"Your Highness, we would be honored if you stayed on with us," Dugray said.

Her father nodded. "Come, we are father and son, now. Call me Petrovich."

Dawson nodded. "I should be delighted to show you about the estate. I believe you will be quite impressed with what you see."

Shearsby coughed and raised his brows at Dawson. "I shall see that the carriage is ready for Prince Sokolov." He looked to the prince. "I am certain you are anxious to get to London before the weather turns for the worst." He walked over and patted the man on the shoulder. "I will send a letter with you. You may stay at Brawly House while you are in London."

Prince Sokolov looked at the duke with narrowed eyes. "What if you should decide to come to London?"

"We will stay at Heatherton House. Not to worry."

Sokolov's expression did not change. "Why should you show kindness toward me? You know little of me."

Shearsby shrugged. "It is in my best interest for you to find a new object for your affections. I will aid those endeavors in any way I can."

Sokolov's glare relaxed, but his sneer still remained. "Very well. I shall depart as soon as my trunks are ready."

"And I shall have your letter of introduction waiting." The duke turned away from Sokolov , muttering to Dugray as he passed. "And a letter on its way by courier. I shall have Billings keep track of him until we arrive after the holidays. Then I shall see him to his ship, myself."

Zia's father clapped his hands. "It seems all is right. Shall we be on our way to Fawnbrooke?"

Shearsby looked to Heathrough, giving him a slight nod. Heathrough motioned Zia's father toward the couch by the fire. "Let us have tea first." Heathrough winked at his brother-in-law. "Let us give the newlyweds a moment to ready the house before you descend upon them."

Zia smiled at her uncle. Had it only been a month earlier when she was afraid to write to this man? Worried he might use her for his own interests? It was amusing how her perceptions had changed over time. Zia looked at Dugray, noting the crinkle around his eyes. Perhaps his was the biggest misperception of all.

Dugray tugged on her hand, pulling her from the room. Once they were alone in the corridor, he pressed her up against the wood paneling lining the walls. He clasped her hands in his and tucked them behind her back. "I know I told your father, but I do not believe I have said it to you yet."

Zia tilted her head to the side. "What is it?"

He leaned down and kissed the tip of her nose. "I love you, Princess Zia Natalya Catherine Petrovich Dawson."

"I know." She ducked her head.

He lifted her chin. "Never doubt my feelings for you. I believe for a moment, in there, you thought I may not love you enough to fight for you."

She dropped her head, ashamed that he had read her so easily.

He dropped one of her hands. Placing a finger under her chin, he brought her gaze up to his. "I blame myself for those doubts. I should have told you before now how I felt. I should have at least told you in Gretna. But I believed if you loved me back, you would see it and I would not have to say anything. I have come to realize the error in my thinking."

He placed a gentle kiss on her lips. "I plan tell you often, Princess, so you never doubt me again. I love you."

Zia released his other hand and threw her arms around his neck. "And I love you, Dugray."

He pulled her to him, releasing all of the stress he had felt just moments ago. He grabbed her by the hand and pulled her toward the entryway. "Come, Princess. We have much to do."

EPILOGUE

The carriage rumbled along the road, the wheels seeming to hit every rut and hole within sight.

Zia glanced out the window and grasped Dugray's arm, squeezing tightly as she peered out. The weather was better, as spring was only a few weeks off. The drop off was hard not to recognize. Dugray rapped on the side of the carriage and it pulled to a stop.

Zia pressed against him, trying to get to the far side of the carriage.

"It is all right. We will not go over. The roads are dry, and the carriage is stopped. I believe it would be good for you to see where the accident happened."

Zia shook her head. "No. I have only just stopped having the nightmare. Surely this will bring it back again."

Dugray wrapped his arms around her. "I am here. I will protect you. It has been over a year." He could feel her trembling within his arms. Perhaps this was not the enlightened idea he had thought it to be. "Come, scoot a little closer to the window. I will not let you go."

Zia looked up into his eyes and nodded. "You saved me from this place once before. Why would I doubt you now?"

She inched her way to the edge and Dugray moved with her, never releasing her from the protection of his arms. She peered out the window, a shudder going from her head to her toes. "Is that part of the carriage? That red wood at the bottom."

Dugray rested his chin on the top of her head. "It is. And that is the tree that succeeded in stopping the carriage."

She took in a shaky breath. "It was a horrible day and a wonderful day all at the same time."

"Oh?" Dugray rapped on the side of the carriage once more and they lurched forward. He could guess at the horror of the day, but what could she possibly find wonderful from that awful event?

A whimper escaped Zia's mouth.

He pulled her onto his lap, scooting them to the far side again. "You did not answer my question."

"It was horrible because I lost Tiana." Zia rested her head against his chest. "I still miss her." She twisted at the buttons on his coat.

Dugray rubbed circles on her back. "I know, Princess."

She took a deep breath. "But it was also wonderful because you found me and saved me from more than just the cold. You saved me from a life of privilege and entitlement."

He chuckled. "It does not sound as if I saved you from such a terrible life. I know many who would be quite happy with a life of privilege."

She swatted at him. "You know my meaning, sir. You helped me see that there is good in people and that there was more to me than my title."

Dawson stopped rubbing her back. "I believe we both learned

much. I learned there is much in life in which to find joy." He resumed the circles. "You also taught me to reserve judgement until I know all the facts."

Zia sighed. "I suppose we both have Tiana to thank." She frowned. "It was her death that started this whole journey." She twisted the pin in Dawson's cravat round and round. "I believe she would be happy with how things have turned out. Do you not agree?"

Dawson grinned and pulled her into him, dropping a kiss on the curve of her neck. "I could not agree more."

AFTERWORD

Dear Reader,

Thank you so much for reading! I hope you enjoyed this story. Dawson has been one of my favorite characters since the very beginning when he and Tad took on an unsavory character at the Liverpool dock.

I always knew that he would get his story, but I knew I needed to have the right woman for him. He needed someone who would stretch his resolve and his patience in order for him to become the man I knew he was. Zia was just such a Lady.

Their story took on many iterations until I got it right, but I think in the end, they are the perfect couple.

Be sure to check out the other books in
Unlikely Match Series
An American in Duke's Clothing
The Baron's Rose

Regency House Party Series
Mistaken Identity
Miss Marleigh's Pirate Lord

Scoundrel's Rake and Rogues Series
Reforming the Gambler

The Belles of Christmas Series
Unmasking Lady Caroline

Happy reading!
Mindy

ABOUT THE AUTHOR

Mindy loves all things history and romance, which makes reading and writing romance right up her alley. Since she was a little girl, playing in her closet "elevator," she has always had stories running through her mind. But it wasn't until she was well into adulthood, that she realized she could write those stories down.

Now they occupy her dreams and most every quiet moment she has-she often washes her hair two or three times because she wasn't paying attention when she did it the first time. Which usually means really clean hair and a fixed plot hole.

When she isn't living in her alternate realities, she is married to her real-life Mr. Darcy and trying to raise five proper boys. They live happily in the beautiful mountains of Utah.

Get up to the date info by visiting my website here.

Sign up to get my newsletter here.

Printed in Great Britain
by Amazon

56383308R00129